Place your initials here to remind you that you have read this book!

THE COP
WITH THE PINK PISTOL

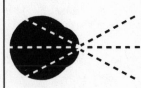

This Large Print Book carries the
Seal of Approval of N.A.V.H.

THE COP
WITH THE PINK PISTOL

GRAY BASNIGHT

THORNDIKE PRESS
A part of Gale, Cengage Learning

GALE
CENGAGE Learning®

Detroit • New York • San Francisco • New Haven, Conn • Waterville, Maine • London

GALE
CENGAGE Learning®

LIBRARY OF CONGRESS CATALOGING-IN-PUBLICATION DATA

Basnight, Gray, 1953–
    The cop with the pink pistol / by Gray Basnight.
        pages ; cm. — (Thorndike Press large print mystery)
    ISBN-13: 978-1-4104-5004-3 (hardcover)
    ISBN-10: 1-4104-5004-X (hardcover)
    1. Policewomen—Fiction. 2. New York (State)—Fiction. 3. Large type books. I. Title.
PS3602.A8467C67 2012b
813'.6—dc23   2012013876

Published in 2012 by arrangement with Ransom Note Press, LLC.

Printed in the United States of America
1 2 3 4 5 6 7 16 15 14 13 12

For my wife, Lisa Weiss,
with appreciation for encouraging my
desire to write.

∎ ∎ ∎ ∎

PART ONE:
THE BURGLARY

∎ ∎ ∎ ∎

1
AND A ONE AND A TWO

"Hey José, there is nothing in this stupid place!"

Vasily Putskya sits on the edge of the rumpled double bed. The tiny apartment is a mess, but that's not entirely his fault. The old woman who lives in it is an even bigger slob than he is. Dirty clothes litter the floor, old newspapers are stacked high, and every tabletop is cluttered with crap, none of it possessing any street value. The bed with a gigantic maple headboard looks like something shipped from Russia when the czar was still on the throne.

Putskya adjusts his Bluetooth headset. "José, I said there is nothing in this stupid apartment. No jewelry. No money. No toys. There is nothing in this place to steal. Nothing!"

"Did you check the freezer?" the voice in his ear asks. "Check the freezer."

Putskya rolls his eyes. He removes his Yankees baseball cap to run his hand over his head in frustration but stops because of the latex gloves on both hands. "Yes, of course I check. Everything. Freezer. Bathroom cabinet. Suitcase under bed. Closet. Shoeboxes. There is nothing. Unless you want something called Crockpot."

"Mierda!"

"Ya . . . govno!"

"I thought that old woman would have a ton of money hiding somewhere," the voice groans.

"Well, you make mistake. There is nothing here. She is poor like Russian peasant poor, which is the poor of all the poor. It is poor as they come." He picks up a book on the bedside table. It is *Crime and Punishment* by Dostoyevsky — in Russian. "Ah, in fact she may really be Russian peasant."

"What?" the voice asks. "Listen, Vasily, there's a lot of traffic out here, you have to speak up for me to hear you, man."

"Never mind! There is nothing here worth stealing. You idiot. You send me into apartment of poor old Russian woman with nothing to steal."

Suddenly the voice in Putskya's ear becomes excited. "Oh, *mierda. Ella entra el edificio. Mierda!*"

"What? Speak English!"

10

"Ella viene. Ahora mismo." Putskya knows something is wrong but he has no idea what. He runs to the door to look through the peephole viewer. The stairwell is dark and quiet. Ready to bolt from the apartment, he rips off the latex gloves and stuffs them into his pocket. He whispers hard and clear into his headset.

"Listen José, I don't speak Spanish. So unless you learn Russian really fast, you have to talk English."

"Vasily, she is coming. She just entered the building. Walk up the staircase so she doesn't see you. Wait for her to go into the apartment, then come back down."

"Govno! Okay." Putskya runs to the telephone concealed under a pile of Verizon and Con Ed bills. Gripping the phone cord, he rips hard, making certain the plastic tab breaks from the jack so the phone will not function. He quietly opens the apartment door, steps out, closes the door, then races up the steps to the small landing, where he stands in silence, waiting for the woman's slow-moving footsteps to reach apartment 7.

"Eh . . ." she mutters, finding that the door pushes open when she tries to insert her key. "Oh *govno!*" she exclaims, noticing the ripped door frame. After she enters her apartment, Putskya quickly darts down the steps, tiptoeing past her broken door as she shouts wildly in Russian.

"Chyort voz'mi . . . Chto za huy . . . Hue-sos!"

Wow, Putskya thinks, *that old woman curses better than I do.* He pauses in front of apartment 4, directly below hers. It too has an ancient wooden door. He could easily pop it open. If nobody is home, he could be in and out in twenty seconds. It'll take the old woman upstairs longer than that to call the police, even if she has a cell phone, which she probably doesn't. It's a little risky, but it's better than going back to José's car empty-handed. Above him, he hears the old woman cursing about shoe-boxes turned upside down and her rifled clothes closet. What's it to her? She's such a slob, what difference does it make? Besides, he didn't even steal anything.

"Hey, Vasily. You okay?"

"Yeah. Hold on. I'm going to try apart-ment number 4 directly below."

"Uh, okay. Be fast, man."

Vasily knocks on the door. Nothing. He knocks again. Still nothing.

"Okay, José. Here goes."

He pulls a crowbar from his right pants leg, inserts the end into the doorjamb just below the deadbolt, and pulls firmly. The wood is so old it barely makes a sound when the lock pops free.

"I'm in," he whispers to his partner.

2
NICELY DONE

"*Muy bueno!* That was one sharp piece of business," José praises. "*Amigo,* you possess a pair of great big brass ones! Did you learn that in Russia?"

"No. America teach me. Everything I know about crime, I learn in America."

They both laugh. They are sitting in José's car, parked at their designated meeting place a block away on Ninth Avenue. They examine the goods stolen from apartment 4. Putskya pulls electronic items from his backpack one at a time, handing each one to José: GPS, iPod, camera, laptop computer, a large pair of army surplus binoculars.

"Nice stuff. Any jewelry?"

"No. I just grab the toys. Oh, and there was this." He turns the backpack upside down, letting hundreds of coins noisily cascade to the floor.

"Oh, he had a coin dish."

"Not anymore," Putskya says, pulling the final item from the backpack, a round brass bowl that he drops to the floor with the quarters, dimes, nickels, and pennies. They laugh again. José leans over to look at the size of the coin pile between Putskya's faded white sneakers.

"Looks like about thirty or forty bucks. Okay," José says, "I can get maybe $500 for the toys. And I messed up bad on the old lady's place, so I owe you one. *Mierda.* I thought for sure that crazy old woman would have a mattress stuffed with money." He withdraws $300 from his wallet and hands it to Putskya. The young Russian takes the money greedily.

"Listen, I'm supervising a Starrhouse move this afternoon," José continues. "Some doctor is moving out of one of those big buildings on the Upper West Side. It's filled with plenty of old rich people. After we park the truck, you can get past the doorman by coming in with us. There may be an easy deadbolt nearby, plus the stairwell is right there. So you can move up and down looking for the easiest door, maybe even get a push-in job. Fifty-fifty split."

"No, no more today. Call me tomorrow."

"*Amigo,* what could be more important than making money?"

15

"Tomorrow . . . nothing," Putskya says.

"Okay, what is more important . . . *today?*"

"Yankee Stadium."

"Yankee Stadium?"

"Yah," Putskya says, adjusting his cap with its official Yankees logo. "There is game this afternoon. And now, with $300 in my pocket, I will buy seat right behind home plate."

"Wow man, I bet you are the biggest Russian-born fan the Yankees ever had." José laughs as Putskya nods, happily accepting the description as a compliment.

As Putskya walks to the nearest subway entrance at Eighth Avenue and Fourteenth Street, he feels the small bulge of the gold ring in his pocket. Sure, he's holding out on José. So what? He takes more risk than the fence does. Besides, the ring will have more value in Russia. In September when he goes back to visit his mother in Moscow, he'll be able to get three times the fence value he can get in New York. That's what big business calls the international exchange rate.

It's only when he descends the subway steps for the uptown A train to make his connection to the D train that will take him to Yankee Stadium in the South Bronx that it hits him hard. What a stupid mistake! He did that second apartment *without* latex.

"Oh *govno!*"

He quickly relives all his moves during the fifteen to twenty seconds he was inside apartment 4. He doesn't remember touching anything, nothing at all, except the toys and the coin dish. And he took all *that* stuff with him.

"Whew," he whispers to himself as the A train roars into the station. "*Sookin syn!* Thank God."

■ ■ ■ ■

PART TWO:
CONNER ANDERSON

■ ■ ■ ■

1
HI THERE

"Conner Anderson? I'm Detective Prima. We spoke on the phone."

"Yes, ma'am. Please come in, Detective Prima."

Donna cradles her clipboard under her arm as she enters apartment 4 at 221 1/2 Eighth Avenue in Greenwich Village. She instinctively gives the front room a quick once-over to ascertain that no threat exists to her personal safety. Not that she's worried, but that's what she's trained to do before entering any space where the circumstances are unknown.

"Your first name isn't Donna, is it?" Conner asks.

"As a matter of fact, it is," she replies, knowing what's coming next. "Just don't call me Prima Donna. Okay? I'm not a prima donna. I am Detective Don-na Pri-ma of the NYPD," she says firmly, emphasizing each syllable in her name and the initials of the New York City Police Department.

Conner Anderson is uncertain how to respond. This woman standing in the entryway of his living room is very sexy, buff, intimidating, and even a little on the masculine side.

Hmm, a lesbian?

Detective Prima examines the damaged door frame. "Basic crowbar job. Nice and easy for him."

"How nice," Conner drawls in his Southern accent, letting the sarcasm linger dramatically. "I wish I'd been here to catch the creep. He'd have gone down the steps wearing his crowbar."

Donna suppresses the urge to laugh at his accent, which reminds her of Bill Clinton's, except that this guy speaks with more honey in his mouth and less hillbilly. She takes in his appearance: male-white, six feet, 175 pounds, black hair, nicely built, perfectly trim with lots of leg.

Molto interessante. But that accent gives him an air of the effeminate.

Hmm, gay?

It's kind of hard to tell. Of course, Bill Clinton isn't gay. But guys this good-looking are seldom straight, and he *does* live in Greenwich Village.

"Don't even think about it," she says, waving him off. "They're ready for that. You walk in on a burglary in progress — it's one of the worst things that can happen. You never know if they've got a firearm. And I promise you they *do* have a knife, which they are happy to use."

"Oh."

"And most of the time they're high. Helps motivate 'em. Believe me, you do *not* want to walk in on a burglar armed with a crowbar and a knife, especially when he just jacked his blood sucking on a crack pipe. The odds of such an encounter ending well are not good."

Conner sighs deeply. "At this point, I'd just like to get my stuff back. In addition to my camera, laptop, iPod, GPS, and binoculars, they stole my father's college ring, which was in a coin dish, along with the coins and the dish too, which they're welcome to keep."

"Right," Donna says, flipping open her clipboard with an official flair. "Let's take a closer look."

Conner gestures with an open arm toward the apartment's interior, inviting Donna to go to work. She does a fast survey of the kitchen and bathroom, making checkmarks on a form. That's what she's there for: to examine the whole apartment — especially the entrance lock — assess the safety of all windows, advise him on the overall security of his apartment, and issue an official police appraisal so he can file it with his insurance company. He's probably hoping to use it to sue his landlord. All crime victims either want to sue somebody or kill somebody.

In the bedroom, she raises the maroon venetian blinds to examine the security of the window, but pauses to look around. The double bed occupies almost all available floor space. There's just enough room for an old-fashioned wrought-iron radiator and a large masculine bureau. The bed frame is polished brass, reminding her of that Bob Dylan song about a big brass bed. The spread is carefully tucked under the pillows and all sides drape perfectly around the mattress and box spring.

Who makes up a bed like that these days? No one she knows, except her Aunt Mary, who lives in Italy. While looking at the bed, Donna allows herself a brief fantasy.

It would probably be easy. And she's never done it in a brass bed.

She shakes the idea from her mind. Southern WASPs are not her style. Of course, one look at this guy and she knew he could be an exception to the rule.

Forget it. I'm in enough trouble already.

Back in the living room, she signs and dates the form, then tears off the yellow copy and hands it to Conner.

"The new deadbolt on the front door is better. But even if you had that before the burglary, they still would have jammed their way inside. It would have been a little more difficult and a little noisier, which is at least some deterrence. These old walk-up buildings are good targets for a smart team because the doors are ancient. There's usually a duo. One guy watches the street, the other goes in with a pull-and-pry bar to pop the lock on these dry-rotted door frames. They usually keep a cell-phone connection between them. The inside guy listens with an earbud, and the outside guy reports if anyone enters, how many, status of the street, that sort of stuff."

"Yeah, they hit my upstairs neighbor the same day."

"That one was probably first. It went good for him, so on his way down the stairwell he saw your ancient door and figured, what the heck, why not a twofer?"

Conner sighs again, deeply.

"What year was this walk-up built?" Donna asks.

"1890."

"I believe it. Listen, I can't tell your landlord to replace the doors in this old building," the detective continues in her tough cop voice, the one that signals she's not interested in a two-way conversation. "But that's how the burglar got in. If you can talk your landlord into installing a metal door with a metal frame you'll be better off. And put a lock on your fire-escape window. A small C-clamp will do the job, something easy to remove if you have to egress in a hurry. Got it?"

"Yeah. Thanks."

"My pleasure." Her smile isn't very big — but it's big enough and suggestive enough to let him know she *could* be interested. If he's not stupid, the next move is his. And if he's straight, he ought to be able to come up with some appropriate and equally obvious response.

"Oh . . . umm . . . uh . . . ," he stumbles.

But before he can get out a coherent word, their ears are assaulted by the scream of a roaring motorcycle zooming up Eighth Avenue. When it's caught at the traffic light directly below, the noise continues to rise from the street with such jarring volume that it rattles the maroon venetian blinds. Donna knows from the obnoxious, high-pitched mosquito-buzz of the pipes that it's not a Hog. It's one of those little crotch rockets, probably a Yamaha, probably with New Jersey plates and probably driven by some suburban white kid from Upper Saddle River, bound for the Lower East Side to buy nose candy for his weekend date.

Conner crimps the yellow form in his hand as he drops onto the couch in the living room. "Will you please write that guy a ticket for noise pollution?" he asks half-seriously in his Southern drawl.

"I'd never catch him. Besides, it's been years since I wrote a noise ticket."

"Fine. How about just leaning out the window and shooting him?"

"Okay, sure. That's different." She pulls up the left cuff of her khaki slacks, revealing a pink revolver strapped snugly to her ankle. "I use this all the time to silence people who annoy me."

"You carry a pink gun?"

Still thinking about the smile she just handed him, Conner stares at the hot pink metallic revolver inside its leather, Velcro-strapped holster attached to Detective Prima's ankle. The smile had taken him by surprise, but it could mean only one thing.

I guess she's not a lesbian.

Conner quickly runs down the list in his

27

mind. She's sexy, she's Italian, she's a cop, she works fast, and with those bulging biceps she's certainly in good shape. Plus she carries a pink pistol.

The loudly revving motorcycle again makes its jarring presence known.

"So what are you waiting for?" Conner asks, covering both ears with his hands. "Please shoot him. I hate those things. They're the worst part about living in the Village."

Donna goes back to the bedroom window, where the view is unobstructed by the fire escape. The Yamaha is lime green. The rider leans into it like an alligator wrestler, revving his motor at the red traffic signal directly below. *I was right,* she thinks — Jersey plates. When the light flips to green, he skids a wheelie from the intersection, screeching away with sonic ferocity.

She changes her mind about the biker's pedigree. He's not a suburban white boy. It's impossible to know with his helmet, but she guesses he's some Pakistani or Indian kid lucky enough to make it past the gate at JFK to blissfully live his idea of true happiness blasting through Manhattan to his busboy job at one of the overpriced yuppiterias around Union Square Park. For him, that lime green motorbike is American paradise between his legs.

"You're letting him get away," Conner calls out.

"Too many forms to fill out if I shoot him. It's not worth it."

Prima glances at the prominent wall decoration over the bedroom bureau. It's a metal-framed poster of a young, blond Laurence Olivier emoting over the skull of Yorick while performing *Hamlet.*

"What's this closet cost you?" Donna asks.

"Two grand for 450 square feet. And for that I may as well be sleeping on the New Jersey Turnpike."

"Rent controlled?"

"Stabilized."

"Not bad," she says, returning to the main room, looking him up and down, and not really referring to his rental status.

"Yeah, when I'm not getting jacked."

His comment makes her smile at him again. "Listen, these guys have been jacking apartments in the West Village and Chelsea all summer. They'll get caught eventually. Either here, or up in the Tenth Precinct."

"That ring is the only memento I have — excuse me, had — that my dad really loved. He wore it every day of his life. And now some little shit is trying to sell it for ten bucks at some flea market in Brooklyn."

"Lower East Side. Or maybe MacDougal Street. Check the jewelry shops around Bleecker too. Sometimes robbery victims get lucky. What kind of ring?"

"Gold with a ruby stone. From Ole Miss, class of '69."

"Did Officer Yance take prints?"

"Yeah. The day after the burglary. She said she got a good one from the hurricane lamp on the desk. And she's certain it's not mine. She told me I might hear from a detective named Tony Sporietto." He pronounces *Sporietto* as though it has fourteen syllables instead of four.

"Yeah, he's a good man. But listen, just some friendly advice — even if they get an ID on these jokers, don't expect much. People don't usually get their stuff back. Break-and-enter guys seldom hold on to stolen goods very long. Believe me, I live in Bensonhurst. I've been hit a few times myself."

"You? Do they know they're robbing a cop?"

"It's hard not to know. My cop hat from my uniform days still hangs in my entryway." Donna is bored with the conversation and wants to return the subject to him.

"Hey, who's the man in the bedroom poster? The one all fired up over that skull?"

30

"Only the greatest actor who ever lived. His name is Olivier."

"He doesn't look Italian."

Her assumption makes it his turn to smile at her.

"What's so funny?" she asks, an edge coming into her voice.

"Oh, nothing. He was a Brit. But he portrayed plenty of Italians in his work: *The Merchant of Venice, Two Gentleman from Verona, Julius Caesar*."

"You're an actor. Figures."

"Yes, I'm on a soap."

"Which one?"

"Vampire Love Nest."

"Never heard of it."

"Hey, wanna go get some lunch or something?"

That was lame. Okay, I guess you're not gay. But I already had lunch. And I can't make this too easy for you.

"Maybe some other time." She gives him the smile one more time. "But now I gotta get back and finish your report."

Donna walks through the miniscule, 450-square-foot, $2,000 per-month apartment with two windows that overlook Eighth Avenue, hectic with motorized traffic. She stops at the front door.

"Listen, I've got to ask. What were the

binoculars for? And don't tell me bird watching in Central Park."

"Well, I wouldn't tell this to just anyone, but I guess you can relate. I've always wanted to be a detective or a secret agent. I read all of Sherlock Holmes and James Bond as a kid. So, when I saw some funny business going on across the street, I bought the binoculars to keep an eye on the comings and goings at the liquor store."

"I'm partial to 007 myself. But then, I like anything old-fashioned. So what's the funny business at the liquor store? And don't tell me kids buying vodka."

"Come here, I'll show you." Donna moves into position next to him at the window. "That's the liquor store down there," he says. "And you see that bar next door, O'Toole's? Well, this past winter, I saw a vintage white Rolls Royce pull up at the light. A big black man got out wearing a full-length white fox fur coat. He walked into O'Toole's, which is strange because O'Toole's is a redneck joint filled with hard-hat types."

"Okay."

"Okay, so I'm watching as this time-warp fashionista from the *Super Fly* days goes into a redneck bar."

"Yeah?"

"So it had to be some sort of dope deal. Right?"

"In the bar?"

"That's my guess."

"Fine," Donna says, already weary of the story. "So why . . . are you watching . . . the liquor store . . . with binoculars?"

"Guess what happened a few minutes later."

"Why don't you just tell me?"

"The big guy in the fur coat comes out. But he comes out of the liquor store next door, instead of the bar where he went in."

Donna strides from the window, more than a little annoyed. "You've been watching too many reruns of *Baretta* on the Nostalgia Channel. Let me tell you something, okay? Don't play private eye or secret agent. It'll only get you in trouble. I know a black man who wears fur coats and you know what he does for a living? He owns a fur coat store." She folds her clipboard folder. This soap opera actor is nice looking. But she has no patience for civilians who think they know the street, especially pilgrims from . . . from — out there.

"Where'd you say you're from?" She tries to imitate his Southern accent, but botches the job. "Was it good ole Mississippi?"

"Tupelo," he corrects, letting a tone of

33

pique bleed into his voice. "It was my dad who attended Ole Miss."

"And how long have you been in the mother of all cities?"

"Two years. What's that got to do with anything? Don't you find it interesting that the guy in the fur coat came out of the store *next* to the bar?"

"No, I do not. So there's a connecting doorway," she lectures him. "Maybe both joints are owned by the same guy. It saves him money on liquor delivery. Let it alone. But if they really are dopers, my advice to you is — do *not* let them see you standing in the window with binoculars. Got it?"

"Got it. But now I have to ask *you* something."

She stops at the wooden door frame scarred from the burglar's crowbar and the locksmith's carvings to install a deeper deadbolt. She anticipates some cornball proposition: how about a drink, how about dinner, what's your phone number?

"Yeah? What is it?"

"Well," he says, "I was just wondering, as an amateur detective myself — if you're a real detective, how come you're doing this kind of crappy clerk stuff?"

She is instantly offended and considers demonstrating just how offended she is, but changes her mind, which surprises her.

"It's none of your business. But I'll tell you. It's punishment. I did something wrong. I'm off homicide case work for a while. Okay?" She gestures with both arms extended, palms turned up as if to say — "so what?"

"And you carry a pink gun in your pants."

"That's right." She pulls up her cuff to display the small pink revolver strapped snugly in its holster. "It's a .38 snubbie. And don't even think about cracking wise. I like it."

"Yeah, but . . ."

"But what?" she barks defensively.

"Well, how'd a macho woman cop like you come to have a pink gun? It's kind of weird. Isn't it against the rules?" He doesn't know it, but he's just pushed the button on her keyboard labeled PISS OFF.

"All right, you want to know? Here it is." Cradling the clipboard in her armpit, she spreads her arms angrily like an umpire calling the runner safe at home. "I don't do face paint. I don't do fingernails. I don't do jewelry. I don't do shoes. And above all else, I don't do jiggle."

"I can see all that."

"As for my weapon — I bought it online. I happen to like it and I don't like anyone making fun of it. Got it?"

"Okay, fine!" Conner barks in return. "Your name is Donna Prima. You are *not* a prima donna. You have a pink gun and you're proud of it."

"That's right."

"And you have strong opinions. On everything."

"Right again."

"And you're very . . ."

"Right yet again," she interrupts angrily. Her volume has increased with each response until she's yelling the way cops instinctively do when they feel their authority is being tested or worse — teased. Donna is proud of her cop voice. But in this case, it's weird. It's like they're having a lovers' quarrel and they don't even know each other.

Conner pauses and resumes speaking in a normal tone.

"All right, then. Just one more question."

Here it comes, she thinks. *Now* he's going to get around to it.

"You any relation to Louie Prima, the band leader?"

Donna is completely disarmed.

"Yeah," she replies, "somewhere back there, fourth cousin three times removed or something like that. You know, big Italian family."

"Yeah," he says, closing the 120-year-old wooden door behind her. "I know."

2
THE SEXY SIXTH

On Eighth Avenue, Donna glances back at O'Toole's Bar and the adjacent liquor store before turning away to walk deeper into the maze of streets that is Greenwich Village, toward the Sixth Precinct and her cubicle on the second floor.

That soap opera actor who talks like Scarlett O'Hara doesn't know the half of it. Civilians should never try to interpret the street; it only gets them in trouble. Besides, knowing what you're looking at can be very tricky. The most innocent-looking problem will get really nasty, really fast, while the most suspicious-looking situation is frequently nothing major — maybe just some middle-aged guys pretending they're not getting old, or some harmless, homeless skell having a bad day. Conner Anderson could never know from looking at that bar, with or without binoculars, that it's actually a long-time police hangout — since the late seventies when a couple of Irish cops retired and opened the joint. But he was right about one thing. It once had a rep as being Irish only, or at least when it came to cops — Irish cops only. Now it's morphed into just another gin mill.

I wouldn't go into that dive if it was the last beer joint in the city, she thinks. *I wouldn't go into that place if a giant helicopter picked up the whole thing, flew it to Brooklyn, and plopped it down on Eighteenth Avenue in Bensonhurst. I wouldn't even go in there if I saw Al Pacino, Robert De Niro, and John Travolta sitting at the bar waiting for someone to talk to. Of course, if Leonardo DiCaprio were with them, that might change things a little.*

She takes the shortest way back to the station, turning east where Fourth Street intersects Twelfth Street, which should be impossible on a grid where all the streets are parallel. But this is the Village. Things and people are different in Greenwich Village; nothing behaves normally here, not even numbers.

Of course, Conner Anderson's speculation is intriguing. What if there really is a narcotics machine grinding away, some middleman delivery operation with a link between a liquor store and a redneck bar? Stranger things have happened. If she could get a leg up on something like that, she could turn it into some fancy media attention, maybe even get her picture in the *Daily News*. And *that* could relieve her of this suspension from homicide work ahead of schedule, get her off the "crappy clerk stuff," as the soap opera actor so unkindly — but truthfully — summarized her situation.

Then there is the man himself. He's on this side of intriguing as well, with looks that remind her of a young Sean Connery. Plus his age is right — 30ish. He's unattached (always preferable). And he works for a living without hurting people. But there is one problem. He's not only an actor; he's an actor with a Southern accent. That's not in line with her cultivated image as a tough Italian-American woman who goes her own way. Aunt Mary would approve of him, but of course she'd approve if her favorite niece settled down with the Naked Cowboy, as long as she doesn't join him in Times Square posing in her Jockey underwear.

Back at the precinct she files the apartment assessment, dupes it to the burglary report in the databank, and logs on to the criminal record file and enters his name: Conner Anderson. What a cornball WASP name. No one from Brooklyn was ever handed such a name. His ancestors probably traveled first class on the *Mayflower* or the *Golden Hind.* They certainly didn't arrive in steerage on the *Niña, Pinta,* or *Santa Maria.*

And look at that. He's lily white: never been arrested. No police record at all. She scrolls down. One speeding ticket a year ago on the Saw Mill Parkway, doing 61 in a 50 MPH zone. That must have been a Sunday when the state troopers have nothing else to do. She turns to the calendar on her desk and flips it back to check the date. Yep, a Sunday. That's a cheesy ticket. She wouldn't write it. But Staties don't care, especially on Sundays. Sunday is revenue enhancement day.

That's it. There's nothing else. Of course his vehicle should not be registered in Mississippi. He's probably doing that to save on car insurance. It's understandable, but risky. The insurer could reject a claim if it learns he's actually a permanent resident of New York.

She logs off the NYPD database and switches to the Internet, which boots directly to ChampionTetris.org. Her latest score flashes: 625,772 at level 20. For her particular game version, the all-time possible max is 999,999 at level 22: the domain of Tetris grand champions. The screen flashes:

Hi Donna,
Would you like to resume your latest Tetris game?

She switches to Google and keys in C-o-n-n-e-r A-n-d-e-r-s-o-n. Several pages of hits immediately generate on *Vampire Love Nest,* a daytime soap about a Park Avenue commune of high-living, blood-sucking zombie sex addicts whose purpose in perpetual death is to wreck the love lives of the living whenever and wherever they can. No major stories single him out, but he is pictured in a promotional photo along with a dozen other men and women posing like junior super heroes, except with fangs instead of capes. She clicks on the main link.

"Hey Donna, how you doing?" It's Officer Jeff Giangola, a patrolman who normally goes off duty before she comes in for the noon shift.

"Hey, Jeff. You're around awfully late."

"Yeah. Me and Sully arrested a pair of lovebirds on Waverly Place. You wouldn't believe it."

"Lovebirds?"

"Yeah. They were doing it on the front stoop. Right there. I mean, doing it *right there* on the front steps of the apartment building at 6:30 this morning with people passing by, locals going to work, dog walkers. By the time we got there, they'd drawn a crowd of gawkers."

"Prostitution?"

"Nope. Mutual consent. I guess they couldn't wait 'til they got home. I mean the guy lived in the walk-up right behind 'em on Waverly. One flight up and they'd have made it safe to the kitchen floor."

"Maybe they were so drunk they thought the front steps *were* that one flight and the front stoop *was* the kitchen floor."

He shrugged. "Yeah, could be. Anyway, after we made 'em do *coitus interruptus,* the guy took a poke at Sully. So I went to the ER at Beth Israel with Sully, then had to come back here to fill out the paperwork."

"Sully okay?"

"Yeah. His wife smacks him harder than that. But he'll be off all next week anyway."

Officer Giangola leans closer into the semi-private space of Detective Prima's cubicle. He lowers his voice. She knows what's coming.

"Speaking of which, since I'm already on overtime, how about you help me extend it by a couple more hours? With Sully out of action, that new chicken coop over on Little West 12th Street will be in the clear."

Donna turns away from her PC to look straight at him, holding firm eye contact, the type of dead-on look that lawyers use to drill witnesses on the stand. "Can't do it, Jeff."

He leans in even closer and speaks more softly. "You sure? You can slip outta here for a while. Captain won't miss you. Your listing on the roster makes you golden. Without homicide case work — you can write your own ticket." The reference to her removal from homicide makes her see red, but she stays calm. She holds a steady, fixed look, a look that is exclusively about the word "no."

"Sorry, Jeff. Can't be done."

"Hey, maybe some other time," he says, easing away from her cubicle and clearing his throat in a showy return to normal volume. "Take it easy, Detective Prima."

She turns back to her PC.

The Website for *Vampire Love Nest* is now fully generated. A show trailer in the middle of the screen begs to be clicked. She clicks it and immediately jumps to turn down the blaring sound effects. The video begins with three sexy vampire women flying south in the night sky above Park Avenue, their lacy nightgowns flapping in the wind. They turn, hover, and land on a penthouse patio, then walk through open French doors into a bedroom where a young man slumbers beneath satin sheets. All women bare their fangs, ready to pounce on the man. He awakens, sits up, and, after a moment, bares his own lustful fangs. The three woman stoop and crawl toward him on the satin bedding as the vampire man receives them with a fang-drooling welcome.

People actually watch this crap? Soaps are supposed to be about those unstable WASPy types. But then, WASPs and vampires are essentially the same thing.

The phone rings two short bursts, which means it's an in-house call.

"De-tec-tive Pri-ma," she announces, with perfect enunciation of every syllable.

"Hey Donna, it's Bill."

"Hello, Captain."

"Listen, come on down here to my office, will ya? I got a man working on something you may be able to help with."

"Sure. Be right there."

She hangs up and descends the staircase to the precinct's main room, where cops come and go as they end a work shift or begin a new one. Unlike the older precinct houses that have the vintage air of old-fashioned police chic, the Sixth has always reminded her of her grade school in Bensonhurst. They were probably both constructed in the same post-war period when prosperity exploded but all charm was lost in the process: brick façade, light-brown slate hallways, dark-green linoleum floors, everything permanently clean but constantly stale and tinged with the odor of astringent with a vague lemony scent.

She passes Giangola behind the sergeant's desk, where's he hitting on a civilian office assistant who smiles back at him. Maybe he'll have better luck with her. The desk sergeant on duty leans into the telephone, talking quietly for privacy.

Where is everyone? Where are the thugs, the perps in handcuffs, the hookers getting booked — all of them cursing and being roughed up by macho cops? There's usually very little of that in the Sixth, and right now there is none at all. The place looks more like a think tank than a police precinct of the NYPD. The Sexy Sixth is actually boring much of the time, at least when compared to the 30th in Washington Heights or the 81st in Bed-Stuy. Maybe she should request a transfer to one of them, to any precinct where there's more action, where cops do more than babysit gay bars and display courtesy, professionalism, and respect to hipsters with tattoos stenciled over their butt cleavage.

The door to Captain Bill Hurly's small office is closed. Knocking once to announce her arrival, she walks in without waiting for a response.

"Detective Prima. Have a seat."

She takes the only available seat, an upright metal chair with a crack in the green plastic cushion. The other chair is a wooden barrel back occupied by a broad-shouldered man with a thick, impeccably manicured mustache. *This one is from the Bureau,* she thinks.

"This is Special Agent Linwood F. Wilson with the Federal Bureau of Investigation," Captain Hurly says.

She extends her hand. "Agent Wilson."

"Officer Prima," he says in response, shaking her hand loosely.

What a prick! That was intentional. No one in professional law enforcement would ever refer to a detective as an officer. This pompous G-man is putting her down for being a female right from the first handshake. She should correct him — let this puffed-up descendant of that drag queen J. Edgar Hoover know that the title on her badge (case duty or no case duty) reads

DETECTIVE. But she decides against it. Not in front of the captain. Besides, let's first find out what's what — then stuff this preening turkey when the opportunity presents itself.

"Agent Wilson is stationed upstate in Port Juttistown, near the big army base up there," Captain Hurly explains, with a noticeable hitch in his voice that tells Prima he's not any more thrilled about this than she is. "He's working with the state PD up there on a case involving stolen government property."

"All right."

"Federal government property."

"All right."

"And it is property the government wants to recover . . ." he eyes Agent Wilson with what Prima believes to be a hint of disdain . . . "very badly. You may be able to provide some assistance to Agent Wilson here while he's in the City."

"May I inquire as to the nature of the stolen property?"

"Detective Prima," Captain Hurly begins, taking off his glasses, "we are not, well that is to say, *I* am not being told the precise nature of the stolen property. Therefore *you* are not being told the precise nature of the stolen property either."

Agent Wilson interrupts in a smug voice. "Let's just say it's very important."

"Well, may I inquire as to where this important property was stolen from?" Prima asks.

Captain Hurly speaks before Agent Wilson can respond. "That much I do know. The property in question was stolen from Dutch Point Nuclear Power Plant. That's the one they built upstate overlooking the Delaware River back during the Carter administration."

The revelation explains why the Feds don't want to reveal too many details, especially to a New York detective who's not even allowed to do case work. She decides to venture one more stab at the nature of the property.

"Animal, vegetable, or mineral?"

"Mineral," burps Agent Wilson, leering at her to let her know it really is important, yes *that* important, in *that* kind of way. *What the hell,* she thinks, *let's keep going.*

"Does it glow in the dark?"

It is one question too many. Except for a small unhappy curl of his lip under that finely coiffed mustache, Agent Wilson makes no response. The captain squirms very slightly in his seat and clears his throat.

"Agent Wilson comes to us with a directive from both the commissioner and the mayor, and they are both responding to a formal request from the governor. So this is pretty fancy stuff. Now, there are two reasons I'm reaching out to you. First, you once worked a case that may have some bearing on this missing federal property thing."

"But I only handled homicides."

"Yes. This particular case involves a homicide — case number H-7211, Mustapha Zizira."

"Sure. Falafel cook at a joint on Leroy Street. Body found in the backroom kitchen. The case is still open as far as I know."

"That's right. We want you to go to the files, revisit the facts, refresh your memory. Then share whatever's there with Agent Wilson here."

Prima likes Captain Hurly. He's a good man, and she knows that he's fond of her — after all, he did go to some trouble to keep her punishment out of the newspapers and away from headquarters at One Police Plaza. Nonetheless, she feels she can't pass up the opportunity to ask a pressing question.

"Captain, will I be allowed to resume working the case?"

"No. The case is now assigned to Detective Sporietto. He is also being asked to share anything with Agent Wilson that he's found since taking over. Just pull together what you can and include your impressions, memories, private suspicions, and whatever else there is."

"In the form of a full report, properly written," Agent Wilson interjects, implying that a woman wouldn't know how to write a proper report.

"And the second reason for pulling me in?"

"Right," the captain says. "Normally we would not — well, the FBI would not — even bother advising us as to the nature of the crime. Normally, we'd just share the report. But the FBI has determined it may need a point man in the Department on this, so — since you once worked a case of interest, and since you are currently available for temporary reassignment, you will be that person. If Agent Wilson requires your services, then you will be available to him this coming week."

"Services?"

"Availability for Q&A, interpreting data, advising on cutting red tape, even partnering with him if necessary. But I emphasize, it is only temporary. One week."

She nods assent. What choice does she have?

3
BORING DESK WORK — PART I

She didn't need to refresh her memory. Captain Hurly knew that. He was just buying her some time, letting her know he didn't like that Fed any better than she did. No city cop worth her badge has any regard for the FBI. Not really. They may go to college and get plenty of training on things like economics or business or computer programming, but they don't know squat about the street.

Where did the captain say this Agent Wilson was stationed? It wasn't Albany, or even Syracuse. What a loser. That's how the FBI punishes agents — it sends 'em to the boonies. And there's no question in her mind — that guy is a loser.

Case #H-7211, Mustapha Zizira, Syrian national, legally immigrated, married an American-born woman of Syrian heritage who works for a small insurance agency, two children, lived in Elmhurst, Queens. Worked at King Falafel, a skeevy Leroy Street hole in the wall that sells pita sandwiches. It's a take-out joint for the lucrative Village pedestrian traffic, with a few tables inside where tribesmen wear white gowns that hang on their plump bodies like nightshirts as they sit around drinking thick Turkish coffee and sucking on Marlboros, which they hold in the middle of their fist so the cigarette never touches their lips.

Zizira was shot in the back kitchen, before the restaurant opened for the day. He was baking a tray of baklava and slicing a lamb shank at the time. Two bullets. One to the chest, one to the head. Marked as a robbery/murder, but nothing was stolen — a tiny fact that tends to stymie the robbery theory.

The other troublesome aspect of the case is the fact that Zizira always kept the front door locked until 10 A.M., opening time. And that's the only door, which means he let the killer in. And *that* means he knew the killer. A full investigation turned up nothing. No gambling debts, no narcotics involvement. The dead guy led a clean life with wife and kids in Elmhurst: just your average, run-of-the-mill immigrant trying to make a new life in paradise.

That's it. That's the whole case. And Detective Sporietto has nothing new. He'd come to the same dead end before moving on to hotter cases. Hot cases get more arrests. As the expression goes, "The colder the case, the older the folder — the merrier the murderer."

There was one other thing. Zizira was AWOL from the Syrian navy. That turned up on his green-card application. But Immigration let him in the door at JFK. If Immigration didn't care, why should the NYPD? Prima remembers her brief conversation with some *piccola merda* at the Syrian consulate to the United Nations.

"What do you ask?" the snooty voice had demanded, very annoyed with her — which had really annoyed Donna. "What do you ask me? Do you ask me — Sir, does the Syrian government send hit men halfway around the world to kill sailors who abandon their duty to their country? If that is what you ask me, my answer is 'No.' No, the Syrian government does not send hit men halfway around the world to kill sailors who abandon their duty to their country."

She prints out all related documents to attach to her report for Agent Wilson. Her last entry on the file was dated almost one year ago, to the day. It reads:

**High probability that victim ac-
quainted with killer on personal
level. Killer suspected to be Syrian
or Middle Eastern man of Arab ethnicity. Motive remains unknown.**

She types a one-page summary, highlight-
ing the facts from the coroner's report,
which explains that the chest shot was fired
from approximately six feet away, while the
head shot was fired from one inch. That's
atypical for a burglar. Burglars tend to shoot
and scoot. This case looked like an execution. That had been her conclusion, even
though she could find nothing to verify it,
nothing linking the dead man to any reason
for getting whacked — no known motive on
the part of the whacker, no known double-
cross on the part of the whackee. But why
tell all that to Agent Wilson, the buttoned-up
FBI man with the finely coiffed mustache?
Let him figure it out for himself.

4
BORING DESK WORK —
PART II

Neighborhood outreach, noise complaints, security assessment, cabaret patrol, prominent display of liquor licenses. It's downright embarrassing — that's what it is. And there's four more months of these moronic missions before she's allowed to resume homicide case work. That's why she volunteers to work weekends, which means overtime pay. But it also means being around cops who get to slap bracelets on perps, yank 'em from the street and toss 'em in the patrol car. If she can't do it, at least she'll be around others who can. It may even mean some small chance that she'll be present when something breaks, something real, something big, something she can respond to that will earn a quicker return to her proper job.

"Buck up, Detective."

It's Ritchie Hennessey, the civilian precinct clerk, who startles her from her daydream. He's toting an armful of mail. "You okay? You look really unhappy."

"Yeah, I'm fine, Ritchie. Just tired of being a former cop."

"Hang in. You'll be back to bangin' heads before ya know it."

"Ritchie, my friend — from your mouth to God's ears. What have you got for me?"

He flips through his stack of envelopes. "Nothing for you. Sorry. This big one is for Sporietto."

She can see that he's embarrassed. He feels bad that he has nothing for her. They both know it's because she's not handling any current homicide cases.

"But it's gonna sit on Sporietto's desk for a while," Hennessey adds. "He's on vacation until the end of the month."

"Didn't know that."

"Yeah. He's in Florida. Wife has family down there with some kind of fancy boat. You know, deep sea fishing. Deerfield Beach, I think."

"My idea of fishing is putting a Mrs. Paul's in the toaster. Hey Ritchie, did you know that? Did you know you can cook frozen fish in the toaster?"

"Wow, Detective," Hennessey says, "you gotta get out more often."

"Seriously."

"I don't think you're supposed to do that. It's an electric hazard. Frozen food is wet."

"Nah, I dry it first with a paper towel."

"Well, you might also try videotaping it for that TV show about stupid stuff people do at home. You might win a trip to Vegas."

She turns back to her computer screen, where the promo for *Vampire Love Nest* has reset. Conner Anderson is in the main lineup, third vampire from the left. Maybe Ritchie is right. Maybe it would be good to get out more often. It's almost Friday night and she's got nothing planned. She contemplates calling Mona Benson to see if she's interested in getting a beer and going to a movie. They went through cadet school together. Mona's now in training to be a desk sergeant at Midtown North.

"By the way," Ritchie calls out, heading for the stairwell exit, "Officer Giangola asked me to give you a message before he left. He says to tell you — no hard feelings."

Donna waves goodbye to the civilian office clerk. She decides against calling Mona. The last time they got together was a month ago for a Yankees game and Mona was all excited over some hot new boyfriend. If that's still on, she will definitely be busy on a Friday night. Donna knows Mona would feel bad and invite her to join them. Forget it. Three's a crowd. And the last thing Donna wants is sympathy.

She waits until Ritchie's footsteps disappear down the stairs before following through on a plan she has just formulated. When Ritchie flipped over that manila envelope addressed to Detective Tony Sporietto, she saw that it was from Officer Yance in the fingerprint lab at headquarters. And she saw the reference to case number B-414. That's Conner Anderson's burglary case.

She pokes her head above the cubicle partition and scans the room. At this hour on a Friday, as the weekend looms, no other detectives are on duty. All mail just delivered will sit on everyone's respective desks until they return on Monday, or until they're called in for some shoot-'em-up or some dead guy. And since Sporietto is on vacation, *his* mail will pile up until the end of the month.

Satisfied that no one else is in the room, Donna retrieves the envelope from Sporietto's desk and opens it. It's a fingerprint report. The lab found a reliable hit on the print taken from 221 1/2 Eighth Avenue, Apartment 4. Print ID'd as belonging to Vasily Leonid Putskya . . . 20 years old . . . Russian born . . . twice arrested . . . three years ago for fencing stolen goods . . . again for burglary in Astoria Heights . . . last known address Markham House, 2199-82 Steinway Street, Astoria . . . last known employment . . . day laborer, Starrhouse Moving Company of Douglaston, Long Island.

That's it. This is the guy who's been hitting apartments in the West Village and Chelsea all summer. There's no question about it — she knows it, senses it, *smells* it. Markham House is a halfway joint for short-term prisoners allowed early release from the jail on Rikers Island. It's in Astoria, right across the bay from the jailhouse. And while there, Putskya was strolling up the street to commit burglary in nearby Astoria Heights. What a dope. Well, his name is Putskya, as in "putz." And the lab made a mistake. Douglaston is not on Long Island. It's in Queens. It's right on the border, but it's on the city side of the border. People from Douglaston have claimed they're from Long Island for so long it's come to be thought of as a part of Nassau County. But cops should know better.

Her phone rings after she returns the manila envelope, carefully resealed, to Sporietto's desk. It's a regular ring, meaning an outside call.

"De-tec-tive Pri-ma," she answers, enunciating each of the five syllables with tough-voiced clarity.

"The Rolls Royce is back."

"Excuse me, sir?"

"This is Conner Anderson. You know, your favorite crime victim. That Rolls Royce is back. The white one."

"I was just thinking about you." She contemplates telling him there may be a break in his burglary case but decides against it. "You're not gawking at 'em with the binoculars, are you?"

"The binoculars were stolen, remember? Listen, I'm just trying to do the right thing. There's probably a million-dollar dope deal about to go down. I can feel it in my Sherlock Holmes/James Bond bones. Or maybe it's machine guns for sale, or uranium-235, or trade in international sex slaves. Whatever. I just thought I'd call you before I call 911."

"What'd I tell you before? Don't play boy detective. Keep your drawers on. I'll be right there." She hangs up and hurries down the internal staircase, leaves her report for Agent Wilson with the desk sergeant, and rushes out into Greenwich Village, teeming with life and traffic in the unusually mild August warmth. After dodging two slow-moving baby buggies and one shuffling panhandler, she turns west on 10th Street, bound for Hudson and north to 221 1/2 Eighth Avenue.

Did she really tell him "keep your drawers on?" Did he really say *"uranium-235"?* What did that closet-case Fed say was stolen from the upstate power plant? Was it some sort of nuclear mineral? Isn't uranium-235 a nuclear mineral?

5
ME AGAIN

The Rolls is still there when she arrives and Conner Anderson is in a state of wild, child-like excitement.

"Did you see the car? It's just been sitting there," he says in an excited voice after opening the door and running back to the bedroom window. "Come and look. No one has come out of the car yet."

"Will you calm down? Yeah, I saw it on the way in," she barks. "You know, when I was on that thing called a street, which is in front of the building entrance, which is where cars are usually parked."

"Right," Conner says, sitting on the end of the bed in front of the window, where he leans forward to peep out. "Did you call in the plates?"

"No, I did not run the plates." She sighs, sits next to him on the bed, and peeks past the venetian blinds, which are turned open just enough to give a clear view of Eighth

Avenue two flights below but without exposing either of them to the world outside. *He's certainly right about one thing,* she thinks. That classic Rolls does look a little suspicious just sitting there double-parked.

"You said no one's left the vehicle yet?"

"Nope. Nobody's come out and nobody's gone in."

Well, she thinks, *if no one has emerged, the occupants are probably conducting their business on cell phones.* Or maybe they're waiting for a second party to arrive. But it's probably nothing. Aside from being double-parked, there's nothing illegal about the antique white Rolls. The good part about all this is that she is now back in Conner Anderson's apartment. And not only that, she's sitting next to him on the foot of his brass bed! It does make for interesting possibilities. And it certainly beats sitting around the Sixth Precinct doing paperwork or going home to Bensonhurst to eat a frozen fish fillet cooked in the toaster.

"Look, we've got some movement now," Conner says.

She leans in closer to the blinds. The driver's door of the Rolls opens, revealing a red-leather interior the shade of a McIntosh apple. A large man emerges from the driver's seat and strides into O'Toole's Bar. She quickly commits his description to memory: male-black, 6'2", 210 pounds, powerful build, hard facial features with eyes that look cautiously in all directions. And the most distinctive thing about his appearance: a full-length white fox fur coat.

Anderson's hunch was right, she thinks. That car is looking more and more like an old-fashioned pimpmobile straight from the set of an old blaxploitation movie, as does the man Conner Anderson calls "Super Fly." A second man emerges but does not enter the bar. Instead, he stands guard beside the Rolls. He is also male-black, 5'11", 180 pounds, muscular build, and very nasty looking. In her judgment, he is definitely armed. Any passing uniform cop witnessing this scene could easily exercise stop-and-frisk authority on either or both.

"You were right," Donna admits. "Something looks funny."

"You gonna call it in?"

Before she can respond there is a scene change. The large black man in the white fur coat emerges from the liquor store next to the bar, looking like an albino Sasquatch. He stands in the doorway and makes a barely perceptible gesture to the man standing guard beside the Rolls, who quickly responds to the instruction by hustling into the liquor store behind the man in white fur.

"See what I mean? Fur-coat man goes *in* the bar, but comes *out* the liquor store."

"Yeah. Like magic. Maybe next time he'll come out of the shoeshine shop three doors down. Now *that* would be a neat trick."

Their eyes are drawn to the small apartment above the liquor store, where a light has flicked on, revealing a man and woman in shadow through a translucent Roman window shade of woven bamboo. The silhouettes of their visibly naked bodies coil around each other as they initiate love making.

"Show time," Conner says.

After a brief moment Donna asks, "You're not a voyeur, are you?"

"No."

"You better not be. Voyeurs give me the creeps."

The two bodies disappear from the window as they move down toward the bed in their apartment. A second later the light clicks off.

Outside, the New York City streetlights are beginning to cast arcs of vague yellow, considerably ahead of dusk. The green-yellow-red pattern of the traffic light directly below alternates with regularity, controlling the flow of everything that moves. The hum of diners and clink of glassware can be heard rising from the restaurant on the ground floor of Conner Anderson's building — Napoli Ristorante Italiano, a small family-owned place. Like O'Toole's Bar, it has been around for decades. Some cops cite it as the location of at least one Mob hit during La Cosa Nostra's glory days. Not just the pre-RICO days, but the *real* glory days, back when working for the Mob was the best job an Italian-American could get. But it must not have been an important snuff job because it was not included on the list of Top Ten Contract Whacks recounted in The History Channel's series on big-time Mafia murders. She makes a mental note to ask her father about it. He's a recently retired Brooklyn firefighter. He never dabbled with the Mob, but with a name like Giuseppe Antonio Prima, and growing up on Carmine Street in Manhattan as he did before moving to Brooklyn, he would know the full story.

While they're focused on the street outdoors, Donna decides they also need something to focus on indoors, lest her attraction for Conner become irresistible.

"Hey, I'm starving," she says. "Let's order Chinese."

"Good idea," Conner agrees.

Within minutes, still sitting on the edge of his perfectly-made-up brass bed with lace bedspread draping all sides, they are both happily eating steamed dumplings and scooping heaps of chicken with cashews onto plates taken from cabinets in his very small but tidy galley kitchen.

"Listen, I've got to ask," she says, working her chopsticks and keeping an eye on the street. "If you're on TV, how come you're in this tiny walk-up? Can't you do better?"

"Funny you should bring it up," he says. "I just bought a condo around the corner on Horatio. The producer of *Vampire Love Nest* lives there. He recommended me to the board. John Carradine used to live there."

"Who's John Carradine?"

"Great actor. Famous movie star. Contemporary of Olivier. He's dead, too."

"Never heard of him."

"Anyway, I move in two weeks. Another two weeks and the scumbag burglar would have been robbing someone else."

"Why didn't you move sooner?"

"Money," he shrugs. "I only got the soap gig this spring. Before that I was doing Off and Off-Off, which don't pay. But there was the one Pepsi commercial I was in. That paid pretty good, and that helped me get onto the soap. So until *Vampire* came along, I mostly tended bar on the Upper East Side. I once served Sean Connery a glass of wine."

"Cool. He's one of my faves."

"Mine too. People say I look like a young Connery."

"Uh, I don't know about that," she says, lying to him. "Besides, Connery talks pretty."

While eating, they keep an eye on the Rolls, which remains unmoved. It hasn't even received a parking ticket for being double-parked and unattended. Nearly twenty feet long, with streamlined running boards, the body is overlaid by the sweep of metal, *real* metal, the way cars used to be made. The windows are smoked to opaque. It's such a pimpmobile it can only be a joke. No real New York City pimp or druggie would ride around in that thing. Not these days, anyway. He may as well run a neon zipper around the length of the car: "b-i-g b-l-a-c-k p-i-m-p . . . p-u-l-l m-e o-v-e-r . . . f-r-i-s-k m-e . . . l-o-t-s o-f d-o-p-e o-n b-o-a-r-d . . . b-i-g b-l-a-c-k p-i-m-p . . . p-u-l-l m-e o-v-e-r."

It finally happens in the declining light of day. Well, it's only natural. She *is* attracted to him, which he already knows; and he *is* attracted to her, which is also apparent. He even makes the first move, and thankfully it is reasonably smooth.

Instinctively, the first thing she does is unstrap the pink Smithie from her ankle and let it plop to the floor. After that, she removes her Polo pullover.

"Why don't you keep your gun on your ankle?" he suggests. "That would be interesting."

She's never heard that one before and she's not sure she likes the idea. Before she can decide if it's creepy, he stops in mid-caress.

"Hey, did you hear that?"

"Hear what?"

"Shh-h-h. There it is again," he says. They lean toward the maroon blinds to peer down at the Rolls, which remains unmoved. She did hear something. It sounded like the muffled scream of a man's voice. "That. Did you hear that?"

Before she can answer, there is another scream, much louder and not at all muffled. It's a man's voice crying out. They both scan the street for the source but see nothing unusual. It sounded close, yet far. Maybe it's in Napoli Ristorante Italiano. Maybe some low-level Mob guy is getting snuffed in the kitchen right now, the first since that unmemorable ice job back in the glory days. What a stroke of luck. If that's the case, she is here, *here,* two flights up and ready to respond. This could be exactly what she's been hoping would happen, the very reason she volunteers for weekend overtime shifts.

"Look," Conner says, gesturing to the apartment over the liquor store. The lights are back on over there. The Roman shade of the bedroom has been pulled up and the man is poking his head past the sill to peer down at the façade of the liquor store and the wider nightlife of Eighth Avenue below. The woman stands naked in front of the apartment's other window as she speaks rapidly on the telephone, making frantic gestures.

Suddenly the air is filled with the sound of distant, muffled cracks.

POP POP POP . . . POP POP POP

The naked woman screams, pivots, and jumps onto the couch as if trying to avoid bullets flying up through the floor before returning the phone receiver to her ear. From their perch in his apartment, Conner Anderson and Detective Donna Prima can hear the woman shout her desperate message: "Gunshots . . . now there are gunshots . . . hurry!"

The man, meantime, has decided it may be best not to expose himself to gunplay. He withdraws from the bedroom window but leaves the shade up, exposing his full-moon hindquarters as he races to his partner's side in the main room, where they both stand on the couch to avoid bullets skyrocketing up from the floor. There follows another, shorter round of cracks.

POP POP POP

The woman screams again and falls to a kneeling position on the sofa. The man does the same as they both tuck throw pillows under them to cushion their naked backsides.

Conner Anderson did not see Detective Prima depart his company on the bed. At some point after the screams, or maybe during the first round of pops, she scooped up her pink pistol and her Polo pullover and moved silently into the living room, bound for the apartment door.

On the street, a solid, broad-shouldered man with an old-fashioned flattop haircut emerges from the liquor store carrying a small set of keys. He springs across the sidewalk without bothering to look at anything except his destination.

"You may want to see this," Conner calls

out. Before she finishes securing the Velcro straps of her ankle holster, Donna darts to the living room window to look past the fire escape, arriving just as the man with the flattop enters the driver's side of the Rolls. He cranks the engine, throws the classic vehicle into gear, and roars off, the Rolls looking like the *Q.E. II* bound for the high seas through a canal of Toyota-made tugboats.

Donna commits his description to memory: male-white, 6 feet even, 190 pounds, angular face, square jaw, old-fashioned crew cut — then finishes the job of securing the holster to her left ankle and pulling on her Polo pullover. Before she can exit, the actor calls out again.

"Police car!" That news — and the familiar noise of the arriving siren accompanied by the halting screech of tires — sends her back to the window. Ah — it's Cicarelli and Gonzalez. They're first on the scene. Good. She rushes from the apartment and down the staircase to join her fellow police officers in the excitement.

6
FINALLY, SOME REAL ACTION

A second patrol car has arrived by the time she's at the scene. Cicarelli and Gonzalez are already inside. A third car screeches to a halt in the middle of Eighth Avenue and is rapidly followed by an unmarked car. This is turning into a real fuss.

She may not be on case work, but that doesn't mean she can't offer assistance. She's still a cop. Cops help other cops. That's the law of cops everywhere. She'd do the same thing even in Yonkers. She withdraws her badge from her belt, then walks into the liquor store.

Three of the four walls are stocked with wine bottles. The fourth wall, the one behind the counter, holds booze. Everything appears orderly. There is no chaos, no indication of violence, no blood on the floor, not a single broken bottle. Two cops are milling about without any apparent urgency.

"Hey, Detective."

"Hey, Officer Gonzalez."

"What brings you here?"

"I was in the area and saw the fuss. What's up?"

"Beats me. There's just one guy in the back room with an old-fashioned boom box."

"Boom box?"

"Yeah. It came over as a 10–30 with shots fired. Sounded like something. But it ain't nothing."

She maneuvers past the gathering crowd of uniformed cops to the small back room, where there is a desk as well as dozens of booze crates stacked up in rows covering the cramped floor. Officer Al Cicarelli is speaking to a male-white . . . approximately 20 years of age . . . 165 pounds . . . average build . . . short brown hair . . . noticeable case of snakeskin freckles on chin, cheeks, and forehead. She knows the look in his eyes — he's scared. But that doesn't mean much; any man would be scared by an army of cops suddenly invading his workplace.

She looks around for evidence of rough stuff that could cause a large black man dressed in a full-length white fox fur and his thuggy-looking bodyguard to disappear. But there is nothing. She also looks for a connecting corridor to the bar next door. There is no sign of it. There's no additional door in either room. Nor is there anything that appears movable so as to reveal the connection. But she knows it exists. It is here somewhere, either in this cramped back office or in the main front room where the wine and liquor are sold.

"Hey, Detective Prima."

"Officer Cicarelli. How's it going?"

"Good. What brings you in?"

"I was nearby and heard the fuss. Gonzalez said it came over as a 10–30?"

"Yeah. Burglary in progress, shots fired." They both look at the male-white sitting in the desk chair, who returns their look with honest bewilderment. She knows something fake is going on. But just like the existence of the hidden passage to O'Toole's Bar, she decides to keep it to herself for the moment. Cicarelli points at the kid. "He says the boom box was blasting. Some gangsta rap thing on the radio. Gunshots. Whatever."

"That's crazy."

"Yeah. The call came from the upstairs apartment. I'm heading there now." He turns back to the male-white with a face full of freckles and speaks in his tough cop voice. "Listen, don't play that thing so loud. Got it?"

"Okay," the 20-something freckle-faced male-white says.

"It's not good for your business or for people who live around here. Understand? Stop with that gangsta crap. Try some golden oldies. Wine drinkers probably prefer golden oldies. Got it?"

"Okay, okay," comes the kid's final defensive response.

The door next to the liquor store that leads upstairs to the apartments buzzes open. Officer Cicarelli and Detective Prima ascend the rickety wooden steps one flight. There are two apartments, one at the rear and one at the front. Cicarelli steps toward the rear door to knock.

"Why don't we try this one first?" Donna suggests, rapping three times on the door of the front apartment as Cicarelli moves into position next to her.

The door squeaks open, revealing a man and a woman, white, both in their late twenties and both wearing matching blue bathrobes tied at the waist.

"Good evening. I'm Officer Cicarelli and this is Detective Prima. Did you place the call this evening regarding shots fired?"

"Yes, sir," the woman says in a worried voice, nodding several times as she holds onto the door like a defensive shield. "It was us. I'm Ann Marnex and this is my husband Charles. Thank you for arriving so quickly." With one hand, she modestly pulls together the lapels of her terrycloth robe, holding them close to her neck.

"Was it a robbery in the liquor store?" the man asks. Donna gives him a once-over from his bare feet to his tussled hair. He's tall and not bad looking.

"No, sir. It appears you heard rap music," says Cicarelli. "Gangsta rap to be specific. Sound effects being played way too loud, blasted by the clerk behind the cash register down there."

"What!" They both gasp. "Music? But it sounded so real."

Cicarelli shrugs. "Yeah. I guess he's got a good sound system. You know, those Japanese can make even small ones sound good these days. They got all those little speakers inside."

"It . . . it just sounded so . . . so real," the woman stammers. "We heard screaming too."

"Yeah, but there's nothing there," Cicarelli says. "That guy down there is clear. I got nothing. And let me tell ya, thank God for those little iPod thingies, because before they came along the kids were all walking around town toting those boom boxes,

Nairobi briefcases, blasting everybody with 'em. Now that's a situation where new inventions actually make life better."

The Marnexes both stare at Cicarelli, dumbfounded by his peculiar lesson on the history of consumer electronics. He tips his cop hat.

"But thank you for your caution. Making the 911 call was the right thing to do. Better safe than sorry. Good evening."

On the way down the rickety steps, Cicarelli leans into Donna to speak in confidence.

"You believe that? Gunshots, my Italian ass. How would they know? It's more like they heard their own fireworks popping off." Before they exit back to the sidewalk, Cicarelli leans even closer.

Here it comes, and she's ready for it.

"Listen Donna, Gonzo is downstairs picking out a selection of adult beverages. How's about you and me spend the rest of our shift over at that new chicken coop the crew set up on Little West 12th? And don't worry, we keep it real clean. We'll have a good time."

"No thanks, Al. I've already had all the good time I can handle for one day."

"I can see that."

"Excuse me?"

"I said, 'I can see that.' "

"You want to explain that?" she demands, letting him know she's annoyed. He taps her elbow.

"Turn around. What's this?" He tugs on the collar at the back of her neck. "Looks like a shirt tag to me. You know, the little white thing that's supposed to be on the *inside* of your clothing."

"Damn!" She'd dressed in such haste, and in the dark, that her Polo pullover is inside out. She elbows Cicarelli in the forearm. "Listen, move over there. Cover the door window with your gigantic backside." He moves to block the sidewalk view while she strips off the shirt, threads it right-side out, and rapidly pulls it back on.

"Very nice," Cicarelli says when the show is over. "Now how 'bout it? You want to join us over at the clubhouse for a little party?"

Prima regains her confidence after a brief fluster of embarrassment, an emotion with which she is generally unfamiliar. "Listen Al, tell me something," she says with a crooked smile. "How's that beautiful wife and those 14 kids of yours? And how's that big house you're paying a mortgage on over in Copland? You know, the tri-level across the Verrazano, the one with five bedrooms on three-quarters of an acre? Everything going okay with all that?"

As they step back onto Eighth Avenue, Cicarelli gives a shrug and acknowledges, "Yeah, all that stuff is going okay."

7
RELUCTANT PARTNERS

Conner Anderson watched the street action with keen devotion from his bedroom window. He hadn't been certain about Detective Donna Prima, who seemed to be sending conflicting signals. He thought it would be safe but was not certain. When he put his arm around her waist — it went fine. And when he kissed her neck — it went *very* fine. Unfortunately, his promising overtures were interrupted by gunshots and the flurry of police activity.

Conner has always been proud of his ability to sense skullduggery. Until now, his biggest success happened when he was 11 years old. After sitting through all three spaghetti westerns in Tupelo with his best friend, he and Louis Toutante were walking home feeling bloated from their two tubs of abundantly buttered popcorn when they came upon an interesting scene. A car was double-parked in front of the Tupelo Farmer's

Bank. The hood was up and a man was leaning into it, tending to some mechanical problem. A second man stood nearby with his hand in his pocket. To Conner, the second man looked suspiciously like a lookout. After passing the bank, Conner pulled Louis behind a parked car on the opposite side of the intersection.

"Phhht," he said, hushing his friend's objections. "Louis, I think that bank we just passed is being robbed."

"Aw, you been watching too much Clint Eastwood," Louis said, waving Conner off.

"No, I'm serious. Look back there," Conner whispered. They took turns peeking over the parked car and through the bank's windows as they studied the scene.

"Don't that remind you a little bit of the robbery scene in *The Getaway* with Steve McQueen?" Conner asked.

"Uh, yeah. Kinda. And maybe a little bit of *Bonnie & Clyde* too."

"So what should we do?" asked Conner.

"Dunno," whispered Louis. "Let's just sit here and watch the big shoot-out when it starts."

A minute later, two men calmly emerged from the bank and entered the double-parked car, followed by the man standing idly at the front. The fourth man, the mechanic, clamped down the hood and got behind the wheel. They all drove off, not only without any shooting, but without any excitement at all.

"That was a bust," complained Louis. "That man under the hood must have been checking his dipstick."

"Yeah," Conner agreed. "Oh well. Fun while it lasted," he said as they walked on, each making fun of the other's foolishness, their chidings carrying them for one jaunty block of laughter until it happened. First came the rattling bell of the bank's alarm, quickly followed by the high-pitched wail of sirens from half a dozen police cars zooming in from all directions.

I was right. It really was a bank robbery!

For the two boys, the development was a bolt of incredulous happiness as they raced in disbelief back to the corner, where they spent the remainder of the day watching the buzz of cops, followed by crowds of gawkers and a trio of TV news cameras.

From that moment, Conner Anderson felt possessed of some greater-than-normal ability to smell duplicity and sniff out clever criminal enterprise. He felt confident that he had a sixth sense, allowing him to understand and accurately interpret a situation at a glance. A natural talent that, had he chosen to go into law enforcement, could have come very much in handy. Of course, being a person of heightened sensitivity also helps him as an actor.

Conner snaps from his daydream when his phone rings.

"Hey Vampire Man, it's me."

"I see all the cops are leaving. What gives?"

"Never mind. Listen, you're an aspiring detective, right? Right. Of course you are," Donna says before he can respond. "So I'm assigning you your first case."

"Okay."

"But don't get any ideas about Batman and Robin. We're not partners. You're only going to be my date. Got it?"

"Got it."

"Okay, so come on down here. You're gonna buy me a beer in that crummy joint."

Donna folds up her cell phone on the street corner, a half block away from the liquor store. While waiting for the soap actor to appear, she watches as the final patrol car departs the scene.

"Detective Conner Anderson reporting for duty."

"Listen, we're just two jokers from the street in search of a Budweiser, okay?"

"Okay."

"Don't say anything about gunshots or

screaming or pimp-mobiles or the two missing male-blacks or anything about any of
that stuff."

"Missing? How can two thuggy-looking
guys just disappear inside a liquor store?"

"Dunno — yet."

"What about the internal connection
between the store and the bar?"

"Didn't see that either."

"You didn't find any stiffs or a connecting
doorway?"

"Nope. That's why we're going into that
skeevy bar. And don't ask for Corona with
a lime, or any of those other bottles your
tribe of WASPy, penny-loafer wearing, blue
blazer, Protestant types drink on Madison
Avenue. Got it?"

"Got it, Chief. Budweiser only."

"Good. Let's go."

O'Toole's Bar isn't much bigger than
Anderson's apartment. Three decades of
exhaled nicotine feed on the walls and ceiling, looking and smelling like mold on
expired yogurt. The bar, the actual counter,
is shellacked to the color of drainage seeping from a sewage pipe. A semicircular arc
on the surface is stripped bare of all colora-
tion by spilled beer and the relentless acidic
effects of barley and malt undergoing glu-
cose fermentation. A classic red-and-white

jukebox angled into a far corner pulsates with the bass chords of "Bad to the Bone" by George Thorogood and the Destroyers, which necessitates either shouting or talking directly into a companion's ear to achieve any communication. Directly above the juke, mounted in a ceiling corner, a clunky old television bulges with blinking refulgence — the Yankees are in Los Angeles, bottom of the seventh, tied with the A's at 3-3.

The bar itself is crowded but not jammed to discomfort; all stools but one are occupied by men leaning into beer bottles, slouching toward one another with rounded sun-burned shoulders or straining backward with fatigued stares at the glaring, convex eye of the 32" Sony Trinitron where Derek Jeter is on deck. Standing room in front of the bar is occupied with blue-jeaned men in Con Ed workshirts. The female contingent is composed of a few tough-looking women in cutoff shorts. Donna and Conner maneuver to the bar, where the detective from Bensonhurst claims the one available stool. Conner, conspicuous in his blue Brooks Brothers button-down Oxford twill shirt and khaki slacks, stands behind her.

"I don't recognize you," the bartender barks without looking directly at either of them while uncapping and shoving a Budweiser at the stout man sitting on the stool next to Donna. He's red-faced with beer and a full day's work in the sun. As for the bartender, except for his attitude, he looks as average as average can be: male-white, medium height, medium build, totally unremarkable appearance.

"I don't recognize you either," Donna shouts past the vibrating rock and roll.

"We'd like two bottles of Bud please," Conner says with a voice trained to project from the viscera, albeit with a Southern accent. The bartender makes no response to the request.

Busy with the details of tending bar, the average man with nondescript features swabs the counter, makes a run on the length of the counter taking money, making change, and tossing gratuities into a large jar labeled "Tips for Tommy O'Toole." After completing the full tour of duty from one end of the bar to the other, including wiping down two highball glasses and making, mixing, and pouring screwdrivers into each of them — he pulls two Budweiser bottles from the cooler, uncaps them, and shoves them toward Conner, still without looking at either of them.

Donna can see without glancing sideways

that the man next to her has maintained his gaze straight ahead, mindful of the brusque disrespect being shown them by the bartender, but also minding his own business. She guesses he's a construction worker and decides he'll suit her purposes just fine.

"Cheers," she says, tapping her bottle with Conner's; the actor lingers uncomfortably behind her and mumbles his response before taking his first sip. Donna turns her bottle perpendicular and gulps down half of the contents before pausing for a breath.

"Sweet," she says, gasping happily, more for the benefit of the red-faced man sitting next to her than for Conner. She tilts the bottle up a second time, empties it, and slams it on the bar.

"Another Budweiser for the unrecognized," she yells to the bartender. She turns to the red-faced man. "Do they have a little girls' room here or do I have to go find a space between parked cars?"

"Naw," the man laughs congenially. "Dehz a john back dere. You know — unisex."

"That could be risky. Well, guess I'll just have to take my chances," she says, easing off the stool as the man's belly jiggles with quiet laughter. "Okay brother, hold my place," she says to Conner. "As Washington once said, 'I shall return.' "

Rinsing glasses in a sink full of treacle water behind the tap handles, the bartender watches her. His eyes follow her past the bar, around the corner, and into a small hallway where she finds two doors. One, labeled TOILET, is a flimsy hollow door; the other is a solid metal door with a security peephole and without a sign, but which may as well bear a warning that reads KEEP OUT. Donna turns the heavy knob on the metal door and pushes.

Che buona fortuna.

Look at that. It's actually unlocked. The door gives way to a small, dark room illuminated only by the shadowy light from the barroom behind her. It's not enough for her to see what's in the room, but there's just enough light to make out the distinct outline of an open floor trap and narrow steps descending to a cellar. She gropes around the door frame, fumbling for a light switch.

"Can I help you?"

It's the mean bartender, the insignificant, Joe-average, male-white who is shouting at her, which annoys her — even if he must shout to be heard over the juke, which has just begun blasting "Baby Did a Bad, Bad Thing" by Chris Isaak.

"I'm looking for the john. Is this it?" she

91

asks, continuing to fumble for a switch inside the darkened room. "Gee, don't you have a light in your bathroom? I mean, women have to see what they're doing, unlike guys, ya know what I'm saying?"

"That's the toilet!" he interrupts, pointing angrily at the adjacent, flimsy door. "That's why it says TOILET on the door — because it's the toilet!"

"Oh. Look at that. Okay, thanks a lot." She eases away from the darkened room as the bartender reaches past her to pull the metal door closed. It clicks shut with a distinctive latching noise. She enters the toilet without looking back.

That's why there's no connecting door. It's because there's a *cellar* connection. Well, those two men are either dead or alive. In all probability they're both dead. But either way, those two male-blacks are down there in a common basement storage area. There's nothing unusual about common cellar space — lots of storefronts share basement storage. Some install cages to prevent neighborly theft, some just draw a chalk line down the middle or run a rope from wall to wall — the shoe store gets the left side, the stationery shop gets the right. The larger cellars have sidewalk entrances. Some even have an electric hoist for lowering deliveries of heavy stuff like pallets piled high with canned goods at the grocery store, or crates filled with dozens of cases of beer at the beer joint, or . . . or . . .

Back at the bar, Conner stands to give the barstool back to Donna. "So what's up with this place?" she asks the red-faced man. "How come the bartender don't like me? I didn't do nuthin'."

"Naw, datz just Billy's way. He's okay. Dis is an okay joint. Kinda old-fashioned, know what I mean?"

"Yeh. I like 'em that way. My favorite bar in Bensonhurst is old-fashioned. I was kinda worried before when I saw that car parked out front. Dunno what it was. Looked like a Rolls Royce or somethin'."

"I didn't see nuthin'. Jus' been here watchin' the game," he shrugs. "I don't pay no 'tention to traffic or people neither."

That's it, she thinks. They're dead. When a giant black man wearing a full-length fur coat in mid-August walks into a redneck joint like this and nobody sees anything — it means the worst. Conner was right about this joint. But she can't call it in. A 911 response has already determined that there's nothing in the liquor store. And there doesn't appear to be anything in the bar. It would look better for her if she could produce some dead bodies. That would be better than calling in a warrant to search for dead bodies when nobody is even reported missing because if nothing came of it — the only result would be more punishment from Captain Hurly, and the trouble could even go over his head to the commissioner. That would be bad — like the song blasting on the juke says, ". . . a bad, bad thing."

Okay, that settles it. There's just too much at risk to call it in. But there's nothing to prevent her from babysitting what may end up as the finest bust of her career to date — and *that* would put her back on the job with plenty of back-pats all around, *including* an atta-boy from the brass at One Police Plaza. It's exactly what she was hoping for, and now it's fallen right into her lap. All she's got to do is nurse it along. Bide her time. Let it pop when it's ready to pop. Her job is to make certain she's there when it does. It's that simple.

"Well, it looks like Mr. Mean Bartender ain't going to bring me another Budweiser. Gee, I wish I knew what I did to that guy. Well, nice talking to you."

The red-faced construction worker nods, laughs quietly, and shrugs.

"Pay the man, brother," Donna says to Conner.

The soap actor drops a ten-dollar bill on the bar that's shellacked to the color of sewer drainage. As the note slowly soaks up spilled beer, Donna notes that the image of Alexander Hamilton vaguely resembles Conner Anderson's profile. Those WASPy types all look like that, she thinks: male-white, thin lips, pointy noises, high brow, smug, holier-than-thou. It's a good thing for him he *also* resembles a young Sean Connery.

8
FULL PARTNERSHIP

"That was a whole lot of fun . . . *sis*."

Disappointed, Conner cannot resist retaliating with sarcasm as they walk east on Fourth Street. "Somehow I expected more than that. Heck, just watching my partner pull out a magnifying glass would have been more fun than posing as your lame brother and watching you flirt with some old hard hat with his Budweiser load on."

"I don't even own a magnifying glass."

"Well, now I know what to get you for your birthday."

"My birthday is a long way off. And when it does arrive — you may be a long way off as well."

"Thanks a lot. That's appreciation for you."

She cuts through the air with both hands, "Shaddup, will ya? Let's walk around the block, just in case somebody's watching."

"Oh, somebody might be tailing us," he

says melodramatically. "Oh-h-h no-o-o. Let's act nonchalant and lose him."

She ignores him. After a few steps of silence, he gives up and asks, "Now what?"

"We go back to your apartment."

"And pick up where we left off?"

"No. Not that I wouldn't like to."

"Then why do you want to go back?"

"To watch. I have to keep an eye on that bar and the liquor store too." She pauses to pull him by the elbow to keep up with her pace.

"Hey, wait a minute." He searches her face for an explanation. "You learned something in that bar."

"Yep."

"What was it? Do I get to know?"

"No. I'm the cop and you're the TV actor, remember? But I'll tell you one thing. You were right. There's something going inside those two joints."

"We've already established that."

"Yeah. But now it's established at a higher level. Before, it was interesting in my mom's church in Far Rockaway. Now it's interesting at the altar of St. Patrick's Cathedral."

Conner is more than a little annoyed but he defers to her tough authority, turning his annoyance into hangdog as he huffs along beside her. She hastens across Fourth

Street, to Twelfth Street, to Greenwich Avenue, then back around to Eighth Avenue, where they turn south.

"I can't imagine what you learned in that bar?" Conner muses. "I certainly didn't see anything interesting. In fact, I hate that joint. It reminds me of every scuzzhole gin mill in Tupelo, maybe even in all Mississippi."

"Relax. You don't need to know what I learned. It's better that way. I know you like playing secret agent or boy detective, but you're not a cop. Besides, working a case with you could only get me in a lot more trouble than I'm already in — *especially* if you get hurt. So if anybody asks, we're just friends. You want to be a cop, join the Auxiliary Unit — you'll get a snazzy uniform and a cop hat. Maybe they'll let you patrol Central Park so you can direct tourists toward Strawberry Fields."

He stops dead.

Uh-oh. Donna can see that she's gone too far.

"Well, aren't you nice. I like that," Conner says, finding some volume to express his own anger. "I put you onto what may be a major criminal enterprise and all I get in return is friendship. And it's not very friendly friendship either."

"Okay . . ."

"And what if I don't want to be friends? What if my apartment is suddenly off limits to the NYPD?"

"All right, relax . . ."

Recognizing that she needs to maintain a balance, Donna stops to consider how to play the situation. She's not allowed to be working *any* cases — not even on her own. And she's already going her own way with her cherished pink Smithie, which is against regulations. If anyone questions her about Conner, she can simply say he gave her a civilian assist. The brass will buy that. It always looks good in the *Daily News* when a civilian helps a cop arrest some perp. The public loves that stuff, too. And the big boys at One Police Plaza always like anything that makes the public love cops.

"Okay," she says quietly, trying to lower the volume on their public verbal fracas, which seems like their second lovers' spat and they aren't even lovers — yet. "Listen, *I* am . . . okay, you *were* . . . okay, *we are* on to something here. Those two men are probably dead. I think they were shot in a common cellar space below those two storefronts. But I can't call it in until I have it nailed good."

His eyes widen in excited approval.

"Whoa," he says, slowly digesting the information. "Bushwhacked in the basement."

"Yeah. When are you back on vampire duty?"

"Monday morning for some exterior scene work. Then late Monday we're back in the studio for a big sex scene that includes flying entrances. Flying is time consuming. It could take a while."

"Good. I ought to" — she sighs — "okay, *we* ought to have something by then. But I repeat, and this is very important, anything happens — we are just friends. I just happened to be inside your apartment. Does that work for you?"

"Well," he slowly responds, enjoying having the upper hand for a change. "Let's see. How about if I tack on a couple of clauses to our contract? First off, no more brother stuff. Okay?"

"Fine," she mumbles.

"And second, if you want use of my apartment for official surveillance, I want to be kept informed. Just keep me up to speed, that's all."

"All right," Donna says grudgingly.

"And third, when you get promoted back to being a big-shot detective, I want my little insignificant apartment burglary flagged with an APB. Make it important. Like if the

Federal Reserve Bank of New York got hit and they stole all the gold in the basement. *That* important. I want my dad's college ring back. And I want the little shit who invaded my 450-square-foot hovel to get beheaded by a giant guillotine right in the middle of Times Square with the mayor of New York pulling the cord to drop the blade on the rat's scummy neck."

There it is, she thinks. All crime victims either want to sue somebody or kill somebody. This one wants blood. She remembers the fingerprint evidence discovered by Officer Yance, the print that fingered one Vasily Leonid Putskya of Astoria. But the burglary takes second place. That's just the way it is. First she has to get the goods in the case of two missing thugs who are probably dead but are not yet confirmed dead — a case that may still turn out to be nothing, which would be very annoying.

"Got it," she says, pretending to be agreeable, a quality that does not come easily. "Okay, let me go over all this just to make certain." She ticks off Conner's list of rules, one on each finger: "No more dumb brother stuff . . . I keep you informed . . . and one burglar scumbag served up for public execution by the mayor."

"In Times Square," he reminds her.

"In Times Square."

"By guillotine," he adds.

"By a giant French guillotine with a blade that rises higher than the ball on New Year's Eve and drops to slice that scuzz-bucket's neck like a hot butcher's meat cleaver through butter pecan ice cream."

"Good. Lead the way . . . *partner.*"

9
SURVEILLANCE

The green-yellow-red pattern of the traffic light blinks through the night that has become wet with a mid-August mist. It's been exceptionally cool for the time of year. The A/C hasn't been needed much since mid-July — a rarity.

Except for the drunk who spilled from O'Toole's Bar, mounted his Harley-Davidson chopper, and roared off at high speed — *on the sidewalk* — nothing of much interest has happened. She'd love to see that biker arrested. There's just never a cop around when you need one.

Conner is bored. During their several hours of watching the street from separate rooms, they've shared a bag of Chips Ahoy, he's made lengthy phone calls to his mother and sister in Tupelo, and he's studied his lines for two scenes in *Vampire Love Nest* to be shot on Monday.

"Did your parents think it was funny?" he

calls out to her, late in the night from his position at the foot of his bed.

"Did they think *what* was funny?"

"Naming you Donna when your last name is Prima."

"My real name is Maria," she shouts from her chair pulled to the window in front of the fire escape. "My full name is Maria-Donatella Prima. And you may leave my parents out of this."

"Maria's a nice name. Why don't you use that?"

"Maybe I'll tell you some day. For now, just stay focused on your surveillance duties."

"That's another thing. Nothing has happened out there. It's really late. So why do we have to stay in separate rooms?"

She's already explained everything she'd seen and suspected in the bar, including her hunch that the cellar is probably a major delivery station for narcotics imported from Afghanistan or Colombia or both. Or it might be a fully operational meth lab. *That'll make a sweet bust,* Donna thinks. She imagines her photo in the *Daily News* and the headline:

Off-Duty Detective
Busts Deadly Village Meth Lab

That'll definitely put her back on case duty. If this thing falls into place just right — it could be like Tetris, when all the little geometric shapes called tetrominoes line up perfectly and the playing screen neatly goes *kah-chunk* as everything glows with success. That would be sweet. If that happens, she could be back on the job by Tuesday morning. Heck, maybe even by Monday afternoon.

"Well?" Anderson shouts.

"Well what?"

"I said, 'Why do we have to keep sitting in separate rooms?' "

"You know why. Surveillance duty is tough. You gotta stay focused — *partner.* Just keep your eyes on both doors and on that pair of metal cellar doors in the sidewalk between the bar and the liquor store. Something's going to break soon."

"How do you know? I never heard of rules that govern when killers get rid of dead people."

"What time is it?"

"3:50."

"Just stay awake. It won't be long now. Last call for booze is right about now. You think they want to work all night? Even dopers and killers want to go home and get some sleep."

Come on, Tetris.

The last bar patrons, a man and a woman, emerge from O'Toole's Bar at 4:05 and stagger east toward Seventh Avenue, probably headed for the IRT subway entrance. Both of them are from Queens or Brooklyn, Donna guesses, and she's prepared to lay even money that at least one of them is a cop, maybe both of them. The door at O'Toole's is left open as they depart, allowing the final song on the jukebox to blast into the night. It is Buckwheat Zydeco's version of "Beast of Burden," which is better than the original by The Rolling Stones.

Yeah, that's what *they're* going to do, she thinks, listening to the lyrics and watching. They're going to draw the curtain and make love just like the song says. The sight of them pulls her concentration away from business. She contemplates giving up and walking into the next room, where Conner is sitting on the foot of his brass bed, peeking at the street through maroon venetian blinds. She could do it. She could just walk in there and make *him* become *her* beast of burden. He wouldn't object. And it *would* be nice. She would certainly enjoy herself much more than sitting here hoping she's stumbled onto something big.

Come on, Tetris.

It's better to resist temptation. Giving in to her natural instincts contributed to her temporary bust back to clerk duty. And it's being on clerk duty that's causing so many overzealous cops to keep hitting on her. They assume she's easy because she feels vulnerable. Bah! What do they know? There's nothing easy about her. They should know that. Maybe if this liquor-store thing turns into a real case, they'll see the error of their thinking. When she's riding high with plenty of praise and atta-boys, they'll treat her with a lot more respect.

Come on, Tetris — DROP INTO PLACE!

"Garbage truck!" Conner shouts.

"Where?"

"Half a block east. It just pulled up. It's just sitting there. The driver's on a cell phone."

"I see it. Okay. It may be something."

"Now we got movement."

"Where?"

"There. Like you said. The sidewalk cellar doors."

The metal sidewalk doors slowly glide open as a beep-beep-beep warning tone sounds, like the back-up warning on a bulldozer. The doors prop fully open and a small rollaway Dumpster gradually rises from the depths below the sidewalk, from the common cellar space below the liquor store and O'Toole's Bar. A man stands behind the Dumpster, riding up on the electric lift. The beep-beep sound stops.

BRUNKK, the lift grinds to a halt at sidewalk level. Then, *BLAMM,* a metal plate drops from the lift and slams to the sidewalk as a ramp. The man pushes the Dumpster from the metal platform down the ramp to the sidewalk. Donna recognizes him. He is Billy Average, the Mean Bartender who wouldn't bring her a second Budweiser. He speaks briefly into a cell phone, folds it, and puts it into his pocket. The garbage truck lurches into gear and chugs forward, its air brakes hissing loudly.

"Disposal of the dead," Conner whispers loudly.

"Damn!" Donna barks. "Okay, the bodies are probably in the Dumpster and they'll soon be transferred to the garbage truck. Where's your car?"

"My car?"

"Yes, your car. You know, automobile. Your vehicle registered in the state of Mississippi. Vanity plate: VAMP NEST."

"How do you know about that?"

"I'm a cop, remember?"

"Right — you're the lady cop with the pink pistol. My car is parked around the block. On Jane Street."

"Let's go."

10
Hot Pursuit (So to Speak)

"What the hell is this thing?"

"My car."

"This is not a car. It's a go-cart."

"It's a Smart Car."

Detective Donna Prima stands on Jane Street staring in disbelief. One of her brothers on Staten Island has a riding mower bigger than this thing.

"Time's wasting. Get in," Conner orders.

The location on Jane Street is between Greenwich Avenue and Fourth Street, a block that seems to have no front entryways, only the rear walls of buildings — thus is always poorly illuminated. The misty rain has stopped, leaving a glaze of wetness coating everything. Conner enters the driver's side and cranks the engine, which sounds like a hedge trimmer. He pushes the passenger door open.

"I said get in. Are we gonna chase the killers, or are you gonna wait for the dead men

110

to reanimate as zombies in pursuit of fresh brains for breakfast, which I happen to know from professional experience will not happen until the next full moon. Come on."

Donna hesitates, wondering if she should explain her situation, confess to him that she has a serious case of claustrophobia. Leaning down, looking at the tiny cabin of the toy car, she thinks *confession* may be the perfect word because this thing is just about the size of a confessional booth, maybe smaller.

Conner is confused by her reluctance.

"*Come on.* You want to find the dead men or not?"

"Yeah, but . . ."

"And do you want to be put back on case work ASAP?"

"Yeah, but . . ."

"Then get in!"

Donna decides against telling him. What's the use in that? She knows she has to get in. So, if she gets in, what's the point in telling him she's a claustro, a *bad* claustro? Does he really need to know that small spaces make her break out in a sweat, that she can't breathe, can't talk, can't think?

She stoops and leans in, but stops when the smallness of the cramped compartment becomes more apparent. "Listen," Conner sighs in frustration, "if you don't get in we're never gonna catch 'em and what's more — you're never gonna get off that crappy clerk duty." It's an irritating threat, but she's in no frame of mind to challenge him.

"Okay, okay. Open all the windows." He pushes the two buttons that make both windows glide down. She slides into the front seat without saying a word, feeling panicky and vaguely nauseated. He reaches past her to close her door.

"Here we go." He guns the hedge-trimmer engine, making the tiny car spring to life. Like a toy poodle leaping to action, it zips from its parking space and glides to the corner of Greenwich Avenue and Eighth Avenue, where Conner pulls over to the curb to spy on the giant garbage truck. It's already gripped the Dumpster and raised it over the cab to dump the contents into the trash bay and is now lowering the Dumpster back to the street.

"Did you see anything fall out?" Donna asks.

"No. We missed that part while you were disapproving of my wheels."

"Merda!" she curses, slamming the back of her fist onto the passenger door.

The forklift claws on the front of the truck

112

plunk the Dumpster to the street with a *CLANG* as Billy Average, the Mean Bartender, disengages it and rolls it back to the sidewalk lift. As soon as the Dumpster is clear of the truck's front end, the driver guns the motor and roars north up Eighth Avenue, sounding more like a freight train than a truck. It is olive green with large black lettering on the side:

FIBONACCI BROTHERS
PORT JUTTISTOWN, N.Y.
& LOS ANGELES, PA.
~ Let Fibonacci Ferry Your Filth ~

They watch it go past, the heavy rear set of double tires making two distinct pairs of tracks in the glaze of misty rain that still coats the street.

"What do we do now?" Conner asks.

"Well, partner," Donna responds, doing her best to overcome all claustrophobic apprehension, "you did pretty good in the surveillance department. How are you in the hot pursuit department?"

"Let's find out," he says, gunning the tiny accelerator pedal, which makes the toy poodle lurch with happy enthusiasm into the middle of the wide tracks left in the wetness by the truck. They reach Eighth Avenue just in time to see the truck turn left on a street in the upper teens. They catch up again just as the garbage truck turns north onto the West Side Highway.

"Where do you suppose he's going?" Conner asks. "I thought the main garbage dump was on Staten Island. That's the other way."

"It is. But it's not the only one."

"Maybe he's headed to the dump that specializes in the disposal of the dead. Where do you suppose that is?"

"New Jersey."

"Is there a designated color for trash containers that separate out recycled dead folks from glass and paper? You know, like *Soylent Green?*"

"That's not funny," she objects. "Remember, I'm old-fashioned. I like old video games like Tetris and I like old movies too. *Soylent Green* is one of my faves. 'It's PEE-pul . . . Soylent Green is PEE-pul-l-l,' " she drawls loudly, imitating Charlton Heston.

"Not bad," Conner says. "That movie should be remade. It'd be better with modern special effects, CGI and all that."

"What's CGI? Computers?"

"Yeah."

"Well, I'd go see it," Donna says. "But you can't improve on perfection. And that computer stuff looks pretty phony most of the time. I don't like phony."

"Hey, is Fibonacci one of the big crime families?"

"Nope."

"You sure?"

"Well, let's see." She counts them out, one per finger. "Bonanno, Gambino, Colombo, Genovese, and Lucchese. Nope, no Fibonacci."

Conner maintains a safe distance from the large truck, yet manages to keep sight of it as it speeds up the West Side Highway. At 57th Street it turns back toward midtown.

"Now what?" he asks. "I guess he's not going to Jersey after all."

"He may be toting dead men, but at least he's obeying traffic laws. No trucks allowed on the Henry Hudson Parkway. He'll take Tenth Avenue and Broadway all the way to the G.W. Bridge."

Half an hour later they cross the Hudson River at the George Washington Bridge and continue south on I-95 for a brief stint before turning west onto I-80. The first hint of sunrise peeks from the horizon behind them as they ride mostly in silence, occasionally breaking the monotony by sharing personal information.

"Did you go to college?" she asks, shouting over the noise of the open windows, which helps distract her claustrophobic anxiety.

"Sure. Didn't you?"

"Sort of. I did two years of criminal justice school. They gave us one of those junior thingies. You know, an associate's degree. But I got my real degree on the streets of Brooklyn. Plus I got the best formal education in the world: OJT at the NYPD. So which one did you go to? Was it — Good Ole Mississippi?" She again botches her imitation of a Southern accent.

He chuckles. "No. I crossed states lines for Tulane."

"What's so funny?"

"It's Ole Miss. My father's alma mater is called 'Ole Miss.' Not 'Good Ole Mississippi.' "

It sounds like the same thing to her and his correction annoys her, but she's not keen on distracting the driver while they're speeding down the interstate in a golf cart with her claustrophobia knocking at the door. So she lets it pass.

"What'd you study?"

"Theatre. I'm an actor, remember?"

"What made you study that?"

"Truthfully?"

"No, lie to me! Of course truthfully."

"Two reasons. First, my looks. As a teenager, I did a lot of local plays and stuff, some dinner theatre. Everybody said I was good and that I'm good looking. You know, the right looks for TV and the movies. Plus I can sing. One thing led to another, so after I finished school I decided to go for the gold. I decided to give it two years in New York and if it didn't work out, then I'd go back to Tupelo and work in my dad's business."

"I had the impression that Papa Anderson has passed on."

"He has. It's a family business. My mom owns my father's half. But Uncle Sammy pretty much runs the show now."

"What kind of business?"

"General contracting. You know, construction — everything from garages to office buildings."

Santa merda!

While he talks, she eyes him in the flashing lights of passing SUVs and noisy 18-wheelers. Who is this guy? He's a college boy, TV actor, easy on the eyes, going out of his way to help her — *and* he comes from money. Hmmm.

"So what's the second reason?"

"Well, I figured if I majored in theatre it would be a good reason not to go back to Tupelo. It's hard enough to make a living as an actor, and you certainly can't do it in Tupelo. So it gave me a good reason for moving. Either L.A. or New York. I chose New York first, and it's worked out pretty well."

"I'm guessing that Uncle Sammy was a problem."

Surprised, he looks over at her in the flashing lights. "Smart," he says with admiration. "You're right. He was a problem. He still is."

"Did he steal the business?"

"He's trying. It's still tied up in the courts, which means my mom is getting cheated out of her half, at least for now. He has this Southern hard hat thing going on. It's kind of like *In the Heat of the Night*. Heck, Uncle Sammy even looks a little like Rod Steiger. And there I was, this local actor and singer, yet legally I was his future business partner because my sister and I are supposed to inherit our share from Mom. That didn't sit too well with him. Plus I had gay friends and stuff. So when I worked on construction jobs, I got called a lot of names, you know — homo, girlie, Shakespeare, and other stuff that I won't bore you with."

"I can imagine."

"And one time when I was working a summer job on a new office building, just as I took off my hard hat to wipe sweat from my neck, a falling hot rivet missed my head by an inch."

Donna considers the story. She's heard it dozens of times, both on the job and over the family dinner table in Bensonhurst. Family partnerships frequently spark disagreements, especially *successful* family partnerships. And disagreements frequently result in family breakups, even vendettas.

"So what are you — like 22 years old?"

"I'm not *that much* of a baby. I did a couple years of construction work in Dad's company before going to college. I didn't go to college until after Dad died and Uncle Sammy became the boss. Plus I've been in New York now for two years."

"So how old are you?"

"Let's just say I'm closer to 30 than I want to be. And besides, if you knew my license plate, why don't you know my age?"

Because she forgot to look at his age when she pulled up his file. That's why. Just like she failed to notice that his car is a wheelbarrow with a lawn mower's motor.

"Why do I know the name Tupelo?" she asks, grateful that the conversation is helping take her mind off her still-churning sense of claustrophobic panic.

"Elvis was born there. He moved to Memphis as a kid."

"You ever try writing a book?"

"Nope. But I'm working on a screenplay."

"Tell me about it," she says, looking for anything to distract her claustro anxiety.

"It's called *Back in Your Life Again*. It's a James Bond movie. But it has to star Sean Connery. It portrays 007 as older, not quite as old as Connery really is. But the character is realistically older, you know — arthritis and stuff. He's forced out of retirement because of a big crisis that only he can resolve. The whole world needs him, that kind of thing. But none of those other guys can play 007. Nobody new either. It's gotta be Connery. That's why it's called *Back in Your Life Again*."

"Sweet. I *like* that. And I bet there's a flashback scene — and *you* plan on playing the young Bond."

"You would win that bet," he says, smiling proudly. "Conner plays young Connery. Has a nice ring, don't you think?"

"Sure does. Hey, I watched the Web promo for your vampire show. All those skinny bitches with pit-bull teeth flying over Park Avenue."

"What'd you think?"

"How come you weren't the one in the penthouse waiting for 'em to join you in that fancy sack?"

He shrugs. "I'm not the lead, I'm a lesser vampire. Like I told you, I've only been with the show since the spring. But characters do get bumped off, or in our case — caught by vampire hunters and written out of the show. That could be good for me. My part could become bigger."

"I guess the pen really is the mightiest," she says. Conner smiles inwardly. He considers telling her the proper word is "mightier," but he lets it go.

"Guess so," he says. "So what about you?"

"What?"

"A book. Did you ever think of writing a book about your police work?"

"Yep. Finished already. I have a reporter friend who's sending it around for me — agents, publishers. I'm waiting to hear back now. It's called *How Stupid People Can Stop Being So Stupid.* The subtitle is *By a Veteran Female Cop Who Ought to Know.*"

"Sounds like a bestseller to me."

"I like to think so."

The trash truck turns off Interstate 80 onto a smaller state highway generally heading northwest. Conner continues to lay back. The truck is easy to spot in the distance so they periodically lag behind by as much as a mile. There's been no indication that the driver suspects he's being followed. Besides, a Smart Car is not exactly the type of vehicle that would cause a thug to worry. Donna keeps her face into the wind of the open passenger window to control her relentless discomfort. She's pleased now to be off the Interstate. Sitting in a Smart Car on a highway that sometimes has twelve lanes of speeding traffic has made her feel like she's skateboarding on a NASCAR track. Several big-rig drivers laughed and pointed; one even laid on the horn and gestured a thumb over his shoulder as he passed the puttering golf cart, a clear signal that said "Get outta here." She guessed the driver of that particular 18-wheeler was Brooklyn-Italian.

The sun is fully up. They're both hungry and would like to stop for breakfast, but they agree it's best to wait. Traffic is light now. But on weekdays, these roads are jammed with heavy traffic heading in the other direction, bound for the G.W. Bridge or Lincoln Tunnel. They're the same roads where a simple fender-bender can mean a two-hour delay in traveling the last two miles into the city. Long work commutes are dumb. Thinking about it now makes Donna regret not mentioning it in her book — even giving it a full chapter. But then, long commutes are so stupid, the subject may even deserve its own book. Hey, that could be a sequel after the original gets published and becomes a bestseller. But of course, even if she becomes a famous author — she'll continue to be a cop. Even after being interviewed by Oprah on her new network, Katie, Tyra, and Ellen. Once a cop, always a cop.

She contemplates the case at hand, running down what she knows so far. There is something very unsettling about the whole situation, but she can't put her finger on it. For one thing, this particular truck is a front loader. It lifts garbage Dumpsters over the cab, instead of from the rear. That means a risk that someone would see two dead bodies come tumbling out, along with all the routine rubbish. That's stupid. When civilians see dead people rolling out of Dumpsters, it tends to generate unwanted interest. Of course, dopers and killers are not known for being the smartest tribe inhabiting the valley. In fact — thugs may even benefit from reading her book, especially the chapter titled "Think Before Doing — Duh."

But it's not just that. There's something else nagging at her, some little detail she's seen or heard but not yet assimilated. It's hammering at her, as if knocking on her door. She tries to unlatch the door and let it walk in, but nothing happens. Maybe it's because of the car — or more precisely because of her claustrophobia. It's her only real issue. Nothing else freaks her. Not the dangers of being a cop, rough-and-tumble stuff with street thugs, wiseguys, high-speed chases, getting shot at, testosterone-charged numbskulls hitting on her — whatever. But an elevator! Now that would set off a bout of sweating that would make her look like she'd just run a marathon. And the idea of getting *trapped* in an elevator — well, that would start with whimpering and she doesn't like contemplating how it could end. For most people, getting delayed in an elevator is a nuisance. For her, it could culminate in a breakdown, cardiac arrest, or worse — it could even lead to the commission of violence, which could be a real problem because she carries a pink .38 caliber Smith & Wesson snub-nosed revolver strapped to her left ankle. Medical doesn't know about the claustro. It's a secret she's managed to keep from the NYPD doctors. Phobias — serious phobias — are things prospective cops are screened for before they get sent to cadet training. Fortunately, they don't check for claustrophobia. Testing to see how long you can stand in an elevator is not a part of cop training.

"Our garbage hearse is turning," Conner says, interrupting her rumination. "Way up there."

"Where are we?" she asks after they follow the truck from the two-lane highway with a posted speed limit of 50 MPH onto a heavily wooded rural road where the first sign they pass reads 45 MPH, followed immediately by a curve in the road where the speed limit drops to 35 MPH.

"Well — we crossed the state line from Jersey back into New York somewhere back there on that two-lane highway. But as for exactly where we are — I couldn't tell you."

"Have we lost the truck?"

"I don't think so," Conner says. "We should be able to spot it on the next straightaway." They round the first curve, the second curve, reach a short straightaway, and slow down again for another series of curves. The speed limit never rises beyond 45. When the road levels and finally stretches out ahead of them — there's no sign of the Fibonacci trash truck. The Smart Car chugs on as Conner and Donna strain their eyes for any indication of the truck or where it may have turned off. Conner keeps an eye on the odometer for almost three miles.

"Well, that's it," he says. "After we turned off into the boonies I was never more than half a mile behind him, and since those curves back there we have now had at least three stretches of half-mile straightaway. I'm certain he's no longer ahead of us."

"Fuoco di merda," she curses, drawing out the words and again slamming the back of her fist on the passenger door. "Okay, double back. There has to be some obvious turnoff, something, anything." The tiny vehicle easily spins 180 degrees in the middle of the road. With the windows down, they look carefully at every turnoff, driveway, and unpaved pathway leading off into the wooded terrain. After two miles of slow backtracking, they get lucky.

"Do you see what I see?" Conner asks.

They watch in the distance as a huge, dark green trash truck emerges from a concealed side road about a quarter mile ahead. The driver stops to look for traffic, enters the road, and quickly picks up speed as the truck pulls away.

"You want to follow him?"

"No. That's not our truck," Donna says. "Make the right turn into the woods where he came from."

"Okay, but how do you know it's not our truck? It looks the same to me."

"Two reasons. That one's got Pennsylvania plates. Ours had New York tags. And look how fast he picked up speed. He's empty. The driver is probably just starting his shift, unless he dumped his load and switched plates in the last ten minutes."

They enter a narrow gravel road, too narrow for two-way traffic, and wind through a wooded area where white-tailed deer graze in the open areas and wild turkey wobble like miniature dinosaurs as they scurry away from the little car's path. At the top of a hill, they pass through a chain-link gate into a wide clearing in the trees where they see several small shacks, a medium-sized Quonset hut housing a garbage truck mounted on blocks, and a small house trailer bearing a sign:

FIBONACCI BROTHERS
PORT JUTTISTOWN OFFICE

In the distance behind the outbuildings, smoke and steam rise from an expansive garbage dump where at least a dozen trash trucks are maneuvering like rats around mountains that rise up from a vast ocean bed of utter contamination, the last stop for the excrement of modern life.

"Jackpot!" Donna exclaims as Conner stops the car at the edge of the clearing, where the whole spectacle becomes apparent with one quick sweep of the eyes.

They both gawk at the scene. But it is not the malodorous open field of debris that steals their attention. It is something else. They stare in amazement at the sudden fortunate turn of events in their efforts at nighttime surveillance and a highway pursuit that has taken them well into the morning. It is there, about 100 yards up the unpaved path, parked directly in front of the decrepit little house trailer — it is the white Rolls Royce.

"Santa Madre di Dio," Donna whispers.

"What do we do now?" Conner asks after a moment, assuming there's no real option except to turn around. They can't exactly go searching for dead bodies in that . . . that . . . whatever it is. And if the driver of the Rolls Royce really is a killer, and he really is sitting at his desk in that skeevoid little trailer office, Conner would rather not be seen riding up to Mr. Fibonacci's place of business in his handy-dandy Smart Car. Showing up for work as a lesser vampire on the set of *Vampire Love Nest* come Monday morning is something he really, really, really wants to do.

"Pull up next to those pickups over there," Donna orders. "That's where the trash-truck drivers probably park their personal vehicles. I'm gonna do a cop thing. You just stay quiet. And try to look the part of my partner. You know, be an actor."

The Smart Car zips into a space between a Toyota Tundra and a Ford F-250.

"I don't want to complain," Conner says, "but in addition to being apprehensive about the outcome of the next chapter in our adventure, I am also sleepy and hungry."

"Me too. Depending on how this thing goes, maybe we can find some breakfast at a roadside diner. Then, providing you do your job, and you're up for it, I'll present you with a little acting award at one of those motels we passed back there."

11
TALKING TRASH — PART I

"Good mornin'. Can I he'p you?"

The receptionist sits on an ancient swivel chair behind a rusty metal desk that could easily date to World War I. She is broad in the beam, like the double tires on the trash truck they've been following, and disproportionately smaller above the waist. Her face is so round it is almost an oddity, her mouth so small it *is* an oddity. Her short Prince Valiant haircut flops evenly around all sides of her circular countenance. Her speaking voice is natural soprano.

This one is home grown, Conner thinks. Perhaps even *inbred* home grown. If she could be teleported into Uncle Sammy's field office in Tupelo, she'd fit right in. Her desk is a messy pile of papers that includes old-fashioned carbon-copied pages, an antique Rolodex, a large open bag of Wise potato chips, and a nameplate reading:

"Yes ma'am, you may be able to help me," Donna says, flashing her badge at the woman. "I'm New York City Police Detective Prima. And this is my associate. We're working a case for the Department of Sanitation. Did a truck just arrive from the city? Straight from Greenwich Village?"

"Yes, ma'am. It sure did. That would be Motty's truck. Number 14. His entire route is all over that Greenwich Village place. He's out dumping now. Let's see." She pauses to finger through a short stack of paper, withdrawing the page pertaining to Motty and truck number 14. "Here it is. Motty's load is assigned to V-88."

"V-88?" Donna asks, noting that Esther Esterhauser betrays no obvious concern about a visit from a NYPD Detective.

"Yep. On the grid." She picks up a wooden yardstick and turns to a large, fading blueprint poster thumbtacked to the wall behind her. "This is a map of the entire dump, and V-88 is, let's see, let's see, there — there it is." She taps the quadrant on the map with the yardstick. "That's way over thatta way," she says, swinging her arm in a wide arc at the general direction as though that is all that is required for anyone listening to know the exact whereabouts of the designated site. "You go down almost to the end, then it's out back thataways." She turns back to her visitors. "Motty's been assigned that general area all week. You want to talk to him? I can text him for ya. No point in calling him, they can't hear a thing when they're in their truck."

Donna glances at the empty office behind the rotund receptionist.

"That's Joe's office. You want to speak to Joe? Maybe you should. He's in the field too, in another truck."

"Joe?"

"Joe Fibonacci. He's the boss."

"Well . . ."

"Is it an illegal refuse case? We get those all the time. Joe'll just tell ya it's not our job to look into the bags, the Dumpsters, or the cans. We just pick 'em up. Any illegality regarding the nature of refuse is purely the liability of the disposing customer."

"Well . . ."

"Of course, we do report it when we see it. Things like propane canisters, car batteries, computers, bags of lead paint removed from school walls, tubs of asbestos, crates full of dead cats. Would you believe it? We get it all. People think because they pay for a private trash service they can just put anything they want in a bag and we'll take it for 'em."

"Well, we were interested in just that one truck. The one driven by Motty."

"Right. He oughta be done soon. He's been on the clock now for over 12 hours. That poor man is ready to go home. If you want to stick around, he should be parking his truck soon. Or I can text him for you. He might feel the vibration if his phone is in his pocket. If not, he'll never know. It's just too noisy in those trucks."

"Don't bother. We'll wait."

"That'll be fine. Care for coffee? The percolator is right there."

"No, thank you," Donna says. "Hey, I couldn't help but notice the Rolls out front. That's some car."

"Oh, yeah. That's Joe's. Don't be too impressed though. It's a '59 model. It looks good, but it nickels and dimes him, or in his case more like hundreds and thousands him. We tease him about it."

"I guess the gas mileage is none too good."

"That too. I think he gets ten miles a gallon, if he's lucky." During her talk with Donna, Esther has taken an interest in Conner, staring at him for long moments as if admiring his good looks. She finally turns to him. "Are you a police officer too?"

"Associate," Conner mumbles, hoping to answer her question without formally claiming to be a cop.

"Have you ever seen a daytime show called *Vampire Love Nest?*"

"Uh . . . I think . . . maybe," he says reluctantly.

"Well, my friend, you need to check it out, 'cause there's an actor on that show who looks just like you — named Conner Anderson."

"Well, thank you for your help," Donna interrupts, managing to speak past a sudden burst of choking. "We'll wait outside for Motty. What's he look like?"

"Oh, you can't miss him. He's a great big black man, very tall. He wears a full-length fur coat, even in warm weather. Solid white."

Conner and Donna are clobbered by the information. They stop mid-stride to stare at each other and turn in unison, displaying slack-jawed astonishment that the corpulent round-faced woman catches and comments on without missing a soprano's note in her happy patter.

"Yeah, can you believe it? We get all types of extravagance in the trash business. It's real ironic. Fancy old cars, fur coats. We've got one driver who's got a sculpture garden in his front yard over in Port Juttistown. He's got art by some famous Eyetalian. I can't remember his name — Bolonie, Bulini, something. And we got another guy who flies biplanes. You know — those things with two sets o' wings and you sit outside, like a convertible. He keeps trying to take me up with him." She giggles. "I keep saying no-o-o, no-o-o thanks, that kind of date I don't need." She giggles again.

"Well, you know, Esther," Donna says in a reassuring tone, "maybe you should reconsider his offer. Because as long as the pilot has both hands on the controls, he won't be getting too frisky while you're up there zooming around the clouds. Know what I mean?"

The receptionist bursts into a song of birdlike giggling. "I didn't think of that. Maybe you're right." She purses her lips and rolls her eyes to the ceiling. "Of course, after we land safely I may be so happy it's over I'd be willing to do just about anything." Donna smiles at the receptionist, who becomes consumed with conspiratorial snickering.

"Well, thanks again," Donna says, exiting the office trailer and pushing Conner out ahead of her before the receptionist can further inspect his familiar good looks.

"You're welcome. I'll tell Joe you were here."

12
TALKING TRASH — PART II

Donna is livid.

"What the . . . who . . . why in the . . ." she stammers, hammering out the words at Conner in an accusatory whisper, leering at him as they walk past the Rolls Royce back to the Smart Car dwarfed between two giant pickups. She can't decide whom to blame: him, herself, or somebody else. "How in the ever-loving world of Frank Sinatra, Dino Crocetti, and Anthony Benedetto did I ever let myself get hooked up with a TV actor, vampire, WASPy boy detective from Good Ole Mississippi?"

"But . . ."

"I told you to back off. Didn't I? Didn't I tell you to knock it off? Didn't I warn you about watching other people's business?"

"But . . ."

"Nothing! That's what this whole thing is. Nothing! A big fat nothing. It's a good thing I didn't go any further last night. If I had called in a warrant . . . I don't even want to think about how much trouble I'd be in now."

"Yeah, but . . ."

"Secret passageways . . . gunshots . . . dead bodies . . . surveillance . . . tailing a trash truck all night in a golf cart."

"But . . ."

"And now I'm standing on the world's biggest pile of stink in Port Jerkheimer or Port Jujube or whatever Port this town is called. I don't even know what state I'm in. Is this Jersey, or what? It may as well be Good Ole Mississippi."

"Are you done? Ahem. Do you remember calling me down to the bar? How about going back to my apartment for surveillance? And who demanded that I get my car? It wasn't my idea. And you still haven't explained how you even knew about my car and . . . if you please . . . my license plate."

"Well . . ."

"And as for how you got into this, I'll tell you how you got into this. When you came into my humble . . . *recently burglarized* . . . abode yesterday to assess my apartment for security, you took one look at me and said 'Hey baby, how about it?' *That's* how you got into this."

"I'd never say 'Hey baby, how about it?' "

Her voice is resentful and offended. But it's not her tough cop voice. It's the real thing, her real voice, the voice of Donna Prima. "That's low class," she says. "And low class is not my style. I simply let you know that . . . I found you . . . interesting."

"Great. I find you interesting too."

"Great!" She saws the air with both hands, her cop voice returning. "Maybe I should have concentrated only on our mutual interest instead of allowing you to play Huckleberry Anderson, the Boy 007."

"Yeah. Maybe we *should* have done that. I'm guessing it would have been more fun than *this*." He gestures to the malodorous dump, where a score of turkey buzzards languidly float overhead. "But we didn't," he continues, "and now we're both here because you made it happen." He taps her sternum with his index finger for effect, which kicks her into a higher gear of cop. When a cop is angry, the last thing you're allowed to do is touch.

"Okay," she shouts, stepping back. "That's enough!"

Conner leans against his Smart Car. Steaming with anger, Donna turns toward the garbage, which begins at a line just behind the trailer office like some creeping ocean surf at a befouled beach. The noxious terrain extends in a curve for what seems an endless length in three out of four directions. She looks at the distant pathways weaving in and out, like a maze in a video game, where the trash trucks maneuver to make their drop. It reminds her of Ms. Pac Man, her second-favorite video game, which is even more old-fashioned than Tetris. Much of the dumped garbage is tamped down into landfill pits, almost to ground level, but some of the little mountains that dot the vast plain are bigger than a house, and the entire compound is enclosed by a ten-foot chain-link fence topped by concertina wire. The sight is so ugly it is difficult to take in; the odor so wretched, it borders on nauseating.

How had she been so wrong? Everything about it seemed to be the real deal. The male-black driving a Rolls Royce who disappeared, gunshots that sounded authentic, the male-white who drove off in the Rolls, Billy Average the Mean Bartender who fit the mold of having something to hide from people he didn't recognize, the common cellar, the trash truck removing evidence. It all seemed to fall perfectly into place, like Tetris on those victorious occasions when all the geometric patterns snugly fit together making the screen go *kah-chunk* and pulsate with congratulations.

Still reeling from disappointment and from her argument with Conner, Donna kneels to take a closer look at an oddly shaped piece of metal poking from the oozing surf of garbage. As she pulls on the protruding metal tip, the bulbous end of the thing snags in the rubbish, causing pieces of shattered glass to fall away. She holds it up and turns it around in her hand. It's a large antique magnifying glass. The handle has been twisted like a candy cane and the glass disc is destroyed, but it's easy to see what it used to be.

What did he say he was going to buy her for her birthday?

Donna holds the metal circle near her face, turns, and looks at the white Rolls Royce through the broken magnifying glass. No. Something is definitely up around here. She has no idea what, but there must be something. There has to be. There just *has* to. It simply cannot be a series of wrong impressions. That would be too many coincidences, and too many coincidences is not the way life works.

She lets the ancient, twisted magnifying glass drop back into the ocean of debris and scrapes both hands together to dust the crud from her palms.

She's made mistakes in the past, plenty of them, the worst being the most recent — the one that hooked her for punishment, removing her from case duty for six months. But that wasn't so much an error of judgment as much as it was a breach of procedure. Sometimes rules should be broken. Unfortunately, there's no rule at the bottom of the list of rules that says, "When necessary — any of the above rules may be broken or simply overlooked." But it should be there. Somebody should tack that rule onto the bottom of every rule list there is.

She sniffs the foul air, smelling more than decomposing rot. She also smells crime — perhaps even serious crime, but so far there's nothing for her to bring to Captain Hurly and certainly nothing to bring to the DA. There's not even anything she can pursue by alternative means, such as tipping off her old reporter boyfriend at the *Daily News* to help flush it out, or bringing in a confidant such as Detective Sporietto to lean on a couple of people — pry it open a crack, then work with him to make it pop.

"Hey, Pink Pistol Lady."

Of course, she could simply issue a report of suspicion and let some other detective eventually get around to looking into both the liquor store and this stinking dump. But then, if she gets any credit at all, it'll be only a footnote. And footnotes don't get detectives off punitive desk duty.

"I said, 'Hey, Pink Pistol Lady.' "

"What?"

"You want to talk to Motty?"

Conner is behind the wheel of the Smart Car, which he's pulled up next to her as she stares at the vast dump. The little car is facing the proper direction to exit through the woods, back toward the paved road.

"Motty," Conner repeats. "You know, the man we thought was a pimp, who we also thought was dead, but who is not dead. I suggest you get in, unless you want to talk to him. Because he's heading our way." She turns to see the approaching trash truck, growing rapidly larger as it emerges from the sea of garbage, being driven be a male-black, lush white fur framing his dark face.

Does she want to talk to him? Maybe she should. And what about this Joe Fibonacci? She pictures herself perched in front of Captain Hurly as he fires questions at her, demanding to know what she was doing in the boonies flashing her badge at legit truck drivers. No. There's no point in talking to either of them. Not now. Not yet. Maybe later if she can come up with something. Choking down her claustrophobia, she rounds the front of the tiny car and carefully gets in as quickly as she can.

"I'm hungry," Conner says, gunning the hedge-trimmer engine as they re-enter the tree line and leave the fetid sea of filth behind them.

13
Code 1063 — Meal Break

"One number-two Good Morning Breakfast over easy, link sausage, whole wheat toast, coffee and orange juice for the lady, and one number-five Lumberjack, baked apples on the side with coffee and tomato juice for the gentleman. Thank you," the waitress says. "I'll be right back with your coffee."

Donna and Conner stare with exhaustion at the rural traffic passing the garishly illuminated diner. The Smart Car is parked in the diner's lot, directly under their window booth. The morning breakfast rush is over. Most of the pickup trucks and older cars have departed. The service station across the street, the only other commercial business on a long stretch of two-lane road, boasts a sign that reads:

GAS & DELLY MART

One of the vehicles getting gassed up is a

Fibonacci trash truck. After inserting the pump hose into the tank, the driver enters the store. When he emerges sipping fresh coffee a minute later, the hose is still pumping gas into the truck.

Conner looks at the truck with interest, noting that the hood ornament is a biplane. "Hey, what about the other guy?" he asks.

"What other guy?"

"The other thug. We know Motty, the fur coat man, is not dead. But he was with that other guy, the one that got called into the liquor store from the Rolls, who we thought was a type of lookout or security guard riding shotgun. Maybe that guy is the one who got killed."

"I know," Donna replies. "I already thought about that. But for now, I have to stand down. I got nothing, a great big fat nothing."

The waitress brings their breakfast on a large tray and distributes the plates. They drink coffee and eat voraciously. When Donna finishes her eggs, Conner offers her a pancake from his tall lumberjack stack, which she accepts.

"You still mad at me?" he asks, digging butter from the mound of little plastic packets the waitress left on the table. He neatly stacks each empty packet, one atop another, until they compose a little tower next to the ketchup bottle. He then pours maple syrup onto the remainder of the stack, which he starts to eat.

"Whaddya mean?" Donna asks, taking the sticky syrup container from him for the pancake he's just put on her plate.

He mocks her Brooklyn accent: "What do you mean 'whaddya mean?' I mean — are you still angry?" At first she has no idea what he's talking about. She pauses with her fork in midair until it sinks in.

"Oh, the thing at the dump? Nah," she says, waving him off with her fork. "Forget it."

"Is that an Italian thing?"

"What?"

"You know — temper. Getting all worked up, blowing your stack, then twenty minutes later you don't even remember doing it?"

"I didn't blow my stack." She jabs her fork in his direction. "Believe me, when I blow my stack — you'll know it."

He considers her assertion that from her viewpoint, she was not angry, or at least not *that* angry.

"It *must* be an Italian thing."

"Why *must* it?" she asks, more of a demand than a question.

"Well, for example, when I get angry, I

mean when I get really boiled about something, which I admit isn't very often you understand, but when I do — let me tell you, I remember it for days. It's an adrenaline thing. Adrenaline pumps you. Sometimes it pumps you so hard it makes you remember stuff for a long time. You know, like when one animal chases down another animal for dinner. Like when a lion runs down an antelope. If the antelope being pursued survives the experience — his adrenaline rush has taught him something important."

"Like what?"

"Like what? Like — he's going to know to steer clear of that lion for all eternity. And furthermore, if that antelope ever gets the chance, even if it's twenty years later, he's going to kill that lion."

Donna shakes her head in disagreement, licking the sticky syrup from her fingers. "Let me tell you something. I arrested a guy once who killed his girlfriend. He strangled her, stuffed her into a cheap trunk he bought at Woolworth's on Sixth Avenue at Waverly. It's not there anymore, there's a bank there now, but never mind that. He poured a bunch of mothballs into the trunk along with her body so it wouldn't stink, which did not work, by the way. When I went to arrest him at his filthy studio apartment on Thompson Street, you know what he said to me?"

"What?"

"Well, he knew my first name. And he said, 'Don't be daft, Donna, you've got it all wrong. I didn't kill her — *she* killed *me*.' "

"I don't get it."

"I didn't either. So I asked him what he meant — since we had the woman's body in the Woolworth trunk, which he stored in the basement of his building and which had his prints all over it — and since he was not dead, but alive and sitting in his filthy little apartment. You know what he said to me?"

"What?"

"He said to me — 'What's the use explaining it to the very person who's got it all wrong?' "

"I still don't get it."

"Well, me either. But in a crazy kind of way it makes sense. What I mean is — it makes sense that it made sense *to him*. In his sicko brain, it made sense not to bother wasting his breath on someone for whom it would make no sense. Meaning me. Know what I mean?"

"Are you trying to tell me I've got something all wrong and there's no point in your explaining the error of my ways because I wouldn't understand?"

"If the sock fits the shoe . . ."

"Well, please waste your breath just this one time. What have I got wrong?"

"Well, for starters, antelopes don't kill lions — ever. And secondly, when I tell you I was not really angry, I mean I was *not* really angry. That's not an Italian thing. It just is what it is."

"I didn't mean to say that antelopes kill lions. Just that an antelope *would* do it — if it could." With his pancakes almost consumed, Conner squeezes lemon into his small glass of tomato juice and drinks it down in one long gulp. Donna watches his Adam's apple bob up and down as he drinks.

"As a lawyer might say — please relate to the court when circumstances could possibly present themselves that would allow an antelope to kill a lion."

"Well, counselor," Conner replies, finishing his juice, "let's say ten years later that old antelope is strolling along in the grassland, happily grazing among the zebras and giraffes, when it suddenly comes upon the lion, the very same lion that tried to kill it and eat it way back when — you know, a whole decade earlier when it got spooked into this eternal memory of caution thanks to the adrenaline rush. Only *now* the lion is old, arthritic, hasn't eaten in weeks, has a fever, can't run, can't do anything except just lie there and wait to become worm food."

"Okay, so?"

"So in that case — the old antelope just might take advantage of the situation. He might just bound right up to that helpless old lion and stomp him. After all, the antelope still has strong legs and hooves that are hard as hammers. So, he just stomps the living crap out of the lion — killing him. He may even talk some trash while he's doing it, saying things like 'You wanted to eat me,' 'You wanted to scare me half to death,' 'You wanted to embarrass me in front of all the other antelope,' 'Take that,' 'And take that.' "

Donna considers the story as she chews the last of her pancake.

"Now *that* is Italian," she says agreeably.

The waitress replenishes their coffee mugs and removes the plates. The hot breakfast has made them feel better but has also made them languid. A teenage girl pushes a woman in a wheelchair to a table near their window booth. When the waitress takes their order, it is apparent the woman has no larynx. She holds an electronic device to her throat to request a number six with coffee. The sound effect is jarring, a cliché robot's voice straight from a 1950s sci-fi movie. Donna and Conner glance toward the sound when they first hear it, but not wanting to stare, they quickly look away.

"Santa Madre di Dio," Donna whispers to herself, looking at the ceiling. "That's it! There's been something about this town that's been nagging at me since last night. It just hit me."

"What is it?"

"What's the name of this town?"

"Port Juttistown. Or at least we're near Port Juttistown. The Fibonacci truck said Port Juttistown, New York, and Los Angeles, Pennsylvania. I didn't know there was an L.A. in PA. I guess we're near one or the other."

"Right, Port Juttistown."

"Would you care for something else?" the waitress asks, passing their booth after taking orders from the woman without a larynx and her teenage companion.

"Tell me something, is there a nuclear power plant nearby?" Donna asks.

"Is there? I'll say there is. It's the biggest employer around. If you don't work there you're pretty much left waiting tables or working at Walmart."

"What's it called?"

"Well, the formal name is Dutch Point. But we just call it 'The Point,' you know, like the way they call West Point 'The Point.' But the people who work there sometimes call it 'Jimmy's House' because President Carter approved it and had it built back during the no-nuke times."

"Where is it?"

"Straight through town, up the main road, then along the river about five miles past the Walmart. Or, if you just want to look at it, there's a scenic pull-over across the river over in Lapa."

"Lapa?"

"Los Angeles, PA. You know, L-A-P-A. That's Lapa. We call it Lapa, but there isn't much in Lapa except a motel, a lumberyard, and plenty of black bears wandering around the woods. Believe me — Port J is bigger. Hey, you two aren't terrorists, are ya?" The jocular question is posed in mock seriousness, but in the current age it is a question filled with righteous civilian caution.

"We were just wondering," Donna says. "We're from the City. And my friend here bet me our breakfast that it wasn't here. He said the nearest nuclear plant was over on the Hudson River, not on the Delaware."

"Nope," says the waitress. "It's right here

in little old Port Juttistown. That's why we all glow in the dark, know what I mean? By the way," the waitress adds, looking at Conner, "you sure do look familiar to me. Are you on TV or anything?"

"Pay the lady," Donna says to Conner as she heads to the ladies' room.

14
THE POINT

"Why do you want to see a nuclear power plant?" Conner asks.

"Can't tell you," Donna replies. "Lousy grunt work I gotta do next week. And trust me, it's not anything I'm happy about."

"So what about that acting award you promised to present in a roadside motel?"

"Oh, that," she says, leaning into the wind of the open window as they emerge on the other side of Port Juttistown, worried about keeping her eggs and sausage inside her stomach where they belong. "That'll have to be postponed. But keep your drawers on. Like Scarlett said, 'There's always tomorrow.'"

"Ugh. I hate that movie."

"*Frankly,* my dear."

"Seriously," Conner says, "The only good part in that movie is when she shoots the Yankee in the face and he rolls down the staircase. Now *that* was a nifty scene."

"Wow, we're in the wilderness already. That wasn't much of a town. If that's bigger than Lapa, then Lapa must go by in a blink. Okay, turn there and head up the river."

"Too bad. I've never done that," Conner says.

"Done what?"

"I've never done . . . you know what . . . in a motel. I've never done that."

"I guess that's a sign of the times. People don't need secrecy much anymore, do they?" She recalls Giangola's story about the couple having front-stoop sex on Waverly Place. "And some don't even need privacy."

"You could be right," Conner says. "I guess it's the influence of TV, the movies . . ."

"Slow down on this next curve."

". . . fashion, advertising, the Internet . . ."

"It should be coming up soon."

". . . maybe the gay movement has something to do with it."

"There it is!" Donna exclaims.

The twin funnel-shaped coolant towers of Dutch Point Nuclear Power Plant appear on the horizon at a sharp jut of land where the Delaware River twists into a narrow dogleg, surrounded by a natural evergreen forest of cedar and spruce trees that rise up the hill from river to road, flanking both sides of the plant. Not far down river, a large sign on the opposite river bank reads:

Los Angeles, Pa.
The True City of Angels

"Did you ever think you'd describe a power plant as being 'beautiful?' " Conner asks. "They really did a good job landscaping that monster."

"Slow down. There's no traffic behind you. Just ride past as slow as you can so I can take a good look at this thing."

Instead of chain-link fencing, the plant's boundary with the road is protected by a serpentine wall of stone, topped by decorative wrought iron. The main gate is a narrow twin-lane break in the wall with a guard house in the median and the standard lineup of built-in spike strips and automated guardrails. A small sign reads EMPLOYEE ENTRANCE.

She can see a second entrance approaching from another direction, winding through the wood of spruce trees along the river. That would be the entrance for industrial delivery by 18-wheelers, Donna thinks. It's unlikely anything stolen from this place would go out the big back door, which probably has more security than the United Nations. If something important went missing from this joint, it was likely done by a single employee who walked out the front door with the goods tucked inside his lunchbox.

There's little more to see. Once the Smart Car is directly in front of the plant, the serpentine wall and landscaped shrubbery obscure everything, even the coolant towers. Only farther down the road does the power plant again become visible in the rearview mirror.

While they're poking past the handsome, well-groomed grounds at no more than ten miles per hour, yet another Fibonacci trash truck comes up from behind and without honking zooms past in the left lane.

"Those things are everywhere around here," Conner says, noting that it's the same truck with the biplane hood ornament that was getting gassed up at the Delly Mart while they ate breakfast.

"Yeah, and the waitress omitted that company from her local job list."

"Huh?"

"You remember," Donna says. "She claimed the only jobs around here are Dutch Point, Walmart, and waiting tables."

"Right. She needs to add Fibonacci to the

list. And judging from what Esther Ester-hauser said — the pay for being a trash man isn't bad: Rolls Royces, fur coats, Italian art, biplanes. And that one that just passed us had a biplane hood ornament. The driver must be the guy who wants to take Esther flying."

Kah-chunk!

Donna looks at Conner, but sees only Tetris as the tetrominoes fall into place. Yes, that's it. Conner has just hit on something important. Driving a trash truck may pay well. Heck, it may even pay *very* well. But it doesn't pay well enough to own Italian art or maintain vintage biplanes. These humps are definitely dealing in the dirty. The only questions are — what kind of dirty and how to nail them? She runs down the prospects: heroin, cocaine, crack, marijuana, methyl amphetamine; or if it's not dope, maybe it's counterfeit currency or guns and ammo. She particularly likes the idea of busting a gang of counterfeiters. That would get the Feds' attention. And it would get her name in the *Times* as well as the *Daily News*. Then again, maybe they're some sort of new-fangled Murder Incorporated. After all, disposal is not difficult for them — the trash truck pulls up, the Dumpster deposits the dead body, quickly and easily. No muss, no fuss. With no body — there're no cops. With no cops — there's no known crime. *Very* efficient.

She eyes the coolant towers receding behind them. Maybe they're even up to no good on some nuclear thing, she thinks, remembering that she's facing secretarial duty to that smug FBI agent with the finely trimmed mustache come Monday morning.

Conner keeps driving beyond the plant. The natural evergreen forest rises on both sides of the road and the air turns cooler. Here in the Catskills, the first autumnal trace of a change in season can already be observed. The deciduous maple and oak leaves are just beginning to show a vague touch of amber on their outer edges — hinting at the orange and red presentation soon to come. About a mile past the plant, the twisting rural road opens onto a long straightaway overlooking the Delaware River on the left and a rocky crag that rises on the right. The view of the river opens wide, revealing flowing water dotted with large rocks and small wooded islands that create white water rapids.

"Beautiful," Conner says. "It's a small-scale version of the Amalfi Coast."

"What's that?"

"*What's that?* It's in Italy! Are you sure

you're Italian?"

"Never mind! Here comes another Fibonacci truck."

"Yeah, it looks like the same one with the biplane hood ornament. It must have turned around."

The trash truck visibly picks up speed in the distance. About a hundred yards away, it edges past the broken white lines dividing the two lanes. About fifty yards away from the Smart Car, it hogs even more of the road until its massive tires perfectly straddle the white lines as it hurtles down the middle of the road toward Donna and Conner.

At ten yards away, the truck veers directly toward the Smart Car, *aiming* for it — intending to slam it, to crush the tiny vehicle and its contents like an aluminum beer can as its giant tires roar forward at 60, 70, 80 miles an hour.

"Dio Onnipotente!" Donna screams.

Microseconds before impact, Conner slams the car's brakes and swerves left, where the car is drawn into a sucking wind tunnel created by the speeding truck, which misses the car by millimeters. Out of control, Conner and Donna glimpse a hyperfast cinematic effect. First, they view the left embankment and the looming river rushing past; after the tiny car gets pulled into the wind tunnel, it's yanked back into a skid, away from the river, where the movie screen changes to craggy mountain wall, which then changes to spinning scenes of rock wall . . . flowing river . . . rock wall . . . flowing river . . . rock wall . . . flowing river . . . and finally — woods, trees, trees, trees, and more trees.

They have avoided being crushed, plummeting into the river, *and* smashing into the rock wall. The car finally stops just beyond the rocky crag on a soft embankment coated with thick green undergrowth of waving ferns adorned with goldenrod and Queen Anne's lace. A large billboard looms directly in front of them, rising from the roadside in a deep cutaway through the trees just inches from where they have come to a stop. The two-foot tall letters on the advertisement fill the windshield like a giant drive-in movie screen. The message reads:

Angel Motel of Los Angeles, Pa.
On the Banks of the Delaware
Clean Rooms - Cheap Rates
Turn Left Ahead at
Dutch Point Bridge
1 Mile to Angel Road

The words are printed over a large image

of a reclining angel, eyes closed, wings folded in. She is sound asleep in a cozy bed with a string of zzz's rising from her slumbering head.

"Madre di Dio," Donna exhales softly, crossing herself.

With adrenaline pumping, they look up at the giant billboard as though it were an altar, a temple of deliverance where the dreams of a guardian angel have put in the fix with God for their salvation.

"Okay," she whispers, as though agreeing with the billboard's message, slowly looking away to examine her miraculously unharmed body. "Okay."

"Okay what?"

"Okay. Let's introduce you to one of America's great pastimes."

"What's that?" Conner asks quietly, looking at the angel.

"What else?" she says, nodding up at the billboard. "The hot-sheets motel."

Without further talk, Conner eases the Smart Car away from the billboard, backs it out of the embankment, moves the PRND stick from R to D, gently guns the hedge-trimmer engine, and picks up speed over the river and through the woods to Los Angeles, Pennsylvania and the Angel Motel on Angel Road on the west bank of the Delaware River.

15
HI MOM, HI DAD —
I'M HOME

As Sunday family gatherings go — it's been fine. Aunt Mary is visiting from Italy and Donna's two brothers and three nephews are all under one roof at her mom and dad's house in Bensonhurst, the same house in which she and her brothers grew up. Her mother, in particular, is relishing every moment of the family reunion. Yet even though the day has been fine, there has been nothing normal about Donna's state of mind. Just 24 hours earlier, she was nearly killed in upstate New York. It was an experience she couldn't shake, couldn't stop thinking about — about how close she came, how tangible the hand of death seemed, and how close it still seemed even as she ate her mother's chicken parmigiana, which she could not look at while eating it.

The other thing she couldn't stop thinking about during the family dinner was him: Conner Anderson. That too was strange,

165

and in an odd way, even more unsettling.

At the conclusion of the family dinner, the clinking of dirty dishes being stacked one atop another punctuates Aunt Mary's chastising litany of Donna Prima, which has been ongoing for several minutes.

"What are you now — 30? Maria-Donatella, I'm talking to you. Did you turn three-oh yet?"

"Close enough, Aunt Mary," Donna replies.

"Well, there you go. That's important."

"What are you talking about? Age is not . . ."

"Children! *Bambini!*" Aunt Mary shouts, hammering the words with a powerful voice and clicking her plump thumb against her middle finger. "That's what I'm talking about — *bambini.* What do you think? Maria, sweetheart, I love you. You are beautiful. You are my favorite niece in New York. My favorite in all America. And I want you to have it all, to fulfill your obligation to God. But you won't be fertile forever. Believe me on that."

Aunt Mary — actually Great Aunt Mary — trots around the table like a referee at a prize fight. Behind her, Julia Prima, Donna's mother, carefully moves the silver tray containing a small mountain of pastries from the side pantry to the main table. Having kept their seats, Donna's two older brothers and their wives immediately help themselves to dessert.

"Kids. Come back to the table for dessert," Julia Prima calls out. "Aunt Mary made struffoli." She turns to the family's houseguest. "Aunt Mary, Donna is married to her job. Someday, she will be the first female New York City police commissioner. Besides, there'll be plenty of time for babies. Women postpone these things nowadays."

Donna appreciates her mother's attempt to intercede. But she knows that Aunt Mary is old-fashioned and doubts the post-dinner conversation at the Prima table is concluded. Donna's three nephews return to the dining room.

"What's struffoli?" the oldest one asks, his nose wrinkled in suspicion.

"Italian honey balls," Julia says. "Aunt Mary made us an authentic Italian dessert." Two of the three kids reluctantly reach across the table to snatch a handful of the sticky, marble-sized honey-covered pastries from the pile. The third boy, the smallest, smirks with disdain and hastens back to the computer in the den, where *Grand Theft Auto* is a bigger attraction than homemade Italian dessert.

"Look at those boys," Aunt Mary says proudly. "They'll be grown and making *bambini* of their own before you." Donna shrugs, escaping to the kitchen, where she helps her mother place the dishes in the dishwasher.

From the kitchen, Donna hears her father trying to change the subject. A retired fire-fighter, Tony Prima knows what it's like to be married to the job. And now that her brothers have children, her mother is satisfied that two of her three children have children of their own. But Aunt Mary? She's a different animal. She visits from Calabria, Italy, for one month every summer. And when she does, Donna can always count on getting hammered on the subject of turning her uterus into a baby factory. Punching out kids is not anything she's ever wanted in life. For her, punching out perps is what it's all about.

Donna returns from the kitchen and sits at the dining room table. Hoping her father's distraction succeeded, she tries chatting with one of her two sisters-in-law on a neutral subject. The tactic does not work.

"And why are you living alone in that apartment?" Aunt Mary asks. "Why don't you live with your family here in this nice big house? It's a waste of good money for you to pay rent. A lovely young woman living alone. It's not safe."

"It's safe for me. I'm a cop, Aunt Mary. I get to shoot people if I want to."

Aunt Mary waves dismissively. "You're a lady. And when men learn of a lady who lives alone — they think only one thing."

Before Donna can answer, her mother intervenes. "Of course she's a lady, Aunt Mary. But she's an *adult* lady," Julia Prima avows protectively. "Besides, she's close enough to us. Right up the street."

"Yeah! Close enough," her father teases, "To come home when she gets hungry. And believe me — my daughter can pack it away without gaining an ounce."

But Aunt Mary will not be distracted.

"So . . . why?" she asks.

"Why *what*, Aunt Mary?" Donna responds.

"You know why what. Why the apartment? Are you entertaining men? Is that why?"

Donna glances at her mother, who smiles with mild amusement.

"Well, I've had a boyfriend or two."

"Tell me about them."

"Well, the last one was a reporter with the *Daily News*."

"And the other one?"

"A lawyer in the D.A.'s office."

"That one is better. And did either of them ask to marry you?"

"No, Aunt Mary. After I had sex with them a couple of times, I kicked them in the ass and told them to beat it."

Her two brothers and sisters-in-law laugh loudly. Her father rolls his eyes while her mother shakes her head, muttering several "Tsk-tsk" sounds of maternal disapproval. But Aunt Mary is not even vaguely amused. After the laughter dies down, she grunts and shoves another handful of struffoli into her mouth while giving Donna a disapproving eye.

"That's not nice," she says.

"I'm a cop, Aunt Mary. Cops are not supposed to be nice. And besides, what about you?"

"What do you mean, what about me?"

"Why are you still a widow after all these years?" Donna asks. "Maybe we need to hook you up with a nice *vecchio*."

"Yeah, Aunt Mary," Tony Prima agrees. "Whatever happened to that gentleman you were seeing in Campo Calabro? The retired train conductor."

"We broke up," Aunt Mary says quietly, looking down at the diminishing mountain of struffoli.

Donna is on the verge of suggesting there

are a lot more fish in the sea when her youngest brother cuts in with the perfect timing of a seasoned stand-up comedian: "What'd you do, Aunt Mary — have sex then kick him in the ass and tell him to beat it?"

The raucous round of laughter at the Prima Sunday dinner table in Bensonhurst is even louder than the first. But Aunt Mary isn't really insulted. Donna knows she even enjoys it. She likes being fussed over. Every time she visits, she scopes out the older men in the neighborhood, always asking who's a widower, who's Italian, and, perhaps most importantly, who has money.

The balance of the afternoon is mostly enjoyable. While helping her mother clean up, Donna makes a veiled reference to having met an interesting man and later asks her mother if her dad would have a problem with a non-Italian. She doesn't mention how *non*-Italian Conner Anderson really is.

"Well, if he did, I'd make certain he got over it real quick," Julia responds, which makes Donna smile.

"Thanks, Mom," she says. "I'm not sure about this one yet, but I'll keep you posted."

In addition to chatting with her brothers, Donna also horns in on her three nephews, making them admit her to their game of *Grand Theft Auto*, which she does not enjoy because it moves too fast and the hand controls are difficult to manipulate. Thinking it to be educational, she logged on and introduced them to Tetris, but she could not convince them that, sure — it's old-fashioned, but it's still fun. They disagreed and called it "boring." When their faces glazed over with foggy detachment, she switched back to *Grand Theft Auto* and left them to their preferred game of simulated violence.

At dusk, her father walks her out to the street.

"You sure you don't want to take some struffoli home?" he asks.

"Trying to watch my weight, Dad." It is a lie. What was left of the struffoli on the large silver plate reminded her of the tray of baklava that Mustapha Zizira was cutting when he was murdered at King Falafel. The little pieces of Mediterranean honey pastry were showered with a mist of blood from the head shot, the *coup de grace*. Normally, the memory wouldn't bother her, but in the morning she'll be revisiting the case with the FBI, and after what happened in the Smart Car, she's still woozy about the whole idea of blood being in places where it doesn't belong.

"You want me to walk you back?" Tony asks.

"No thanks, Dad. Besides, I'm the one with the gun. And I've got to stop at the grocery anyway." She doesn't tell him that she needs to buy Eggos for breakfast. "Dad, did you make many mistakes? On the job, I mean?"

"Sure," he shrugs. "All the time."

"Did you get punished?"

"Not really. Nothing serious. Basically just a black mark or two early on, for things like being late to a night shift. I was driving once when the old ladder truck dropped the transmission and slammed into an overpass embankment. But nobody cared. In fact, they thanked me because we got a new truck out of it."

A police siren wails a block away. Donna holds her gaze on her father as he turns to watch the passing cruiser speed through the nearest intersection.

"Listen, sweetheart, I know what's on your mind. Your violation is nothing to be ashamed of. You did your time in uniform. You got your shield at an early age because you *earned* it. You'll be back on homicide duty soon. And when you're back, there'll be no need to look back. It'll be like it never happened. Just keep relying on your instincts like you always have and you won't go wrong."

"Thanks, Dad."

"May I tell my detective daughter something else, on another subject?"

"Sure, Dad."

"You know, when you return to full duty, it may be best if you put that pink .38 in your underwear drawer and replace it with your regulation piece."

"I know, Dad. Don't worry, I will. I'm just enjoying it for the time being."

After kissing her dad good night, Donna watches her father reenter the house in which she grew up. *He beat she system,* she thinks. Retired at 62 without serious injury; he's still in good health, happily married, Mom's fine, they have no debt and nothing to worry about. That's the way it *should* be done. Somehow, she's not so sure that's the path she's destined for. Things are different for cops. There's just so much more stuff that can get in the way. Stuff like — the reason she's currently on desk duty.

New York City Police Detective Maria-Donatella Prima turns from her family home and walks toward the neighborhood grocery and her apartment two blocks away as nightfall descends on Bensonhurst.

■ ■ ■ ■

Part Three:
The Vampires of
the Banalities

■ ■ ■ ■

1
KING FALAFEL — PART I

"First of all, I read your report this weekend, and while it was reasonably thorough, I am sorry to say — it omitted one very important detail. Second — and maybe precisely because of that omitted detail, it is too bad you allowed H-7211 to go cold so quickly. That is very unfortunate. You see, Officer Prima, this case I am working on has the attention of the very highest authority."

There is it again: officer. Merda!

Agent Linwood F. Wilson turns around to look at Donna sitting like a loser in the back seat of the unmarked black Ford Town Car as it chugs through eastbound traffic in Greenwich Village. "The very *highest* authority."

Donna ignores the preening boast that glides past the neatly trimmed bush on Wilson's upper lip. "Did you contact Detective Sporietto to see if he's got anything new? He's been on it since I was reassigned."

"I spoke to him on the phone. Squat!" Wilson asserts without turning his head. "That's what he's got — squat. Besides, he's out on vacation until the end of the month, and not very talkative."

The driver slams the brakes to avoid hitting a bicycle messenger weaving in and out of traffic as he speed-pedals his way down Seventh Avenue. Agent Linwood F. Wilson and the driver, Agent Ian A. Holm, both mutter curses.

Do all FBI agents use their middle initials?

"Can't this city do something about those kamikaze bastards?" Holm complains, giving Donna an exasperated look in the rearview mirror. "We don't have anything like this in DC." His forehead is suddenly dotted with scores of tiny beads of sweat.

"You don't have a lot of stuff in Washington that's tolerated in this city," Wilson adds with equal disdain, looking at a pair of gay men in hot pants strolling hand in hand down Seventh Avenue, "or in Albany or Binghamton or any other upstate city where I work for that matter." He shakes his head in disbelief.

The black Ford emerges from the largely residential rabbit warren of the Village. They are bound for the commercial heart of Greenwich Village, where the partisan tribes of humankind work cheek by jowl in every available cubbyhole in every narrow street and alley selling the marketable stuff of their commercial ethnicity, be it cannoli, knish, tikka, tamale, bouillabaisse, boquerones, wasabi, wonton . . . or falafel.

Prima knows she is supposed to ask *Golly sir, what important detail did I miss . . . please excuse me . . . how may I make it up?*

Very highest authority.

Yeah, right. That's how Special Agent Linwood F. Wilson got assigned to Port Juttistown — by taking orders from the *very highest authority.* Captain Hurly knows this guy would just waste his time if left on his own in the big city. *That's* why she's assigned to him — to prevent him from getting roughed up by some kitchen full of Syrians for not knowing the rules. Once they learn he's not from Immigration — they lose all fear. This part of the Village might be the commercial crossroads of the planet, but it's not a place for sassy, out-of-town white boys to shake badges at Latinos or wave the stars and stripes at Arabs.

Donna decides to ignore his complaint about the report. The Town Car is caught at a red light at Bedford Street. A giant Fibonacci trash truck chugs by in front of them. The sight of it sends a shiver of

179

unpleasant memory through Donna. It not only reminds her of Saturday's close call, but also that she has some unfinished business relating to that upstate trash company. The lettering on the side of the truck passes by like a ticker-tape headline . . .

"F-i-b-o-n-a-c-c-i B-r-o-t-h-e-r-s P-o-r-t J-u-t-t-i-s-t-o-w-n N-Y & L-o-s A-n-g-e-l-e-s P-a Y-o-u D-o t-h-e N-u-m-b-e-r-s . . . L-e-t F-i-b-o-n-a-c-c-i F-e-r-r-y Y-o-u-r F-i-l-t-h."

"Hey, look at that, Agent Wilson," Donna says. "That truck is from your upstate town."

"Yeah. I know Fibonacci."

"Is he a Mob guy? The Mob is heavy into the trash business. Well, they are here in the City, at least."

"Nah. The district office in Albany had me look into his books. He's clean. Donates to every Republican candidate in the state. Good hard-working American."

Dolce! Thank you, Special Agent Linwood F. Wilson.

She leans forward from the back seat.

"Leroy Street is the next left. King Falafel is half a block up, on the left. We can park at a yellow curb, also on the left." The two FBI agents exchange knowing looks and chuckle. "What's so funny?" Donna asks.

180

They trade a second look of amusement.

"Well," Agent Wilson says, turning to her with a smirk, "it's just that it sounds like everything in this town is on the left."

Dolce Gesù! Working with these clowns is turning out to be just as much fun as she figured it would be.

At mid-morning, King Falafel is already doing a bang-up business selling darkly powerful Turkish coffee and toasted pita bread covered with garlic butter. Many customers are students from nearby NYU. Others are waiters and cooks on their way to countless restaurants about to open for lunch but who stop here before moving on to jobs at the café, diner, brasserie, sandwich shop, or pizza parlor. Carryout customers sit on benches chained to either side of King Falafel's front order window. The interior is unchanged since Donna last saw it while working the case: a few tables for customers who linger over coffee and, this morning, two roly-poly men wearing full-length nightshirts which, curiously, look like seersucker pinstripe cotton. In violation of the law, they chain-smoke Marlboros by sucking on their fist. Donna recognizes one as the owner of King Falafel. He is the younger of the two, about 45, and the pudgier of the pair. His eyes show a keen alertness, a natural intelligence. He is clean shaven and wears orange flip-flops too small for his protruding, fat feet.

"Hello, Samir. How's business?"

"Hello Lady Capp-itahn. Bah. Business not good. You catch killer yet?" He does not rise from his chair but speaks in an agreeable manner as he eyeballs the two men in their light brown business suits. "Business would be better if I had my Syrian cook back. These Egyptians, they just don't make good chefs like Syrians make good chefs."

"I'm not a captain, Samir. I'm a detective. These gentlemen are from the FBI. They would like to have a look at the kitchen. Not the small one in the front window, but the big one in back where Mustapha was murdered. Would that be all right?"

"Okay," Samir says without hesitation, gesturing to the back. Wilson and Holm meander away without speaking. Donna can see Samir does not like them. They have violated protocol by not showing even a hint of courtesy. Once they're out of sight, Samir looks at his older companion with curiosity. Donna guesses the older man is either Samir's father or father-in-law. Samir looks at Donna with the same questioning face he gives the older man. Prima shrugs as if to say, "Don't look at me, I don't know any more than you do." Samir reads her body language and turns into himself, thinking deeply and drawing smoke from his fist, then blowing it absently to the floor in great clouds of exhaust.

The cook in the small kitchen at the front window works rapidly in his small space, maneuvering his arms like a finely trained surgeon making rapid moves, shaking deep fryers, slicing tomatoes, steaming espresso, receiving money, making change. One inept move and the hot oil spills or the finger gets sliced instead of the tomato.

After a moment, Samir looks up again as though he's discovered an answer to a puzzle.

"Ah!" he says to Donna. "I see. They look at more than Mustapha. They look . . ." and with both hands he pantomimes the meaning for *big, bigger, biggest.*

Donna responds with a shrug containing a vague acknowledgment that he could be right.

"Samir, tell me something." Donna speaks in a manner of confidentiality. "Do you think Mustapha could have been into any . . . well . . . nasty stuff? You know . . . like any anti-American stuff?"

"No."

"Are you sure?"

183

"Sure I sure. I know him. He care only — family. Has house — Queens. Wife — beautiful. What he care about that? He come America — work. Nothing. He no care."

"Well, did you ever talk to him about it? I mean, everybody talks about this international war stuff, about Muslims hating America and all that. What did he say about that? What were his opinions?"

"No. Nothing. He no care. He just live, work. I no care. My house — up." Samir points to the ceiling where his wife and three children live in the apartment above King Falafel. "My family — up. My work — down." He gestures outward with both hands to indicate the limited space of King Falafel, his small piece of American paradise. "What I care? I live — up, I work — down. Life simple for me." Proud of his words, he sucks on his fist, looking squarely at Donna and blowing thick smoke into the air.

Donna believes him. She never felt that Mustapha Zizira was involved with a terror plot or ever had any desire to be involved in one. If he was, she missed it by the widest margin imaginable when she was on the case. Her reading was and still is — murder by an acquaintance over some personal vendetta. But even that avenue remains a mystery. Except for his AWOL status, Zizira was clean.

Returning from the kitchen, the two FBI agents approach Samir's table. Without asking, Agent Wilson sits while Agent Holm stands where he can watch the two Syrian men, as well as monitor the customers drinking Turkish coffee and eating hot pita toast. One bedraggled-looking man with bushy grey hair ravenously eats a large plate of rice pilaf with an oversized spoon, scooping it to his mouth like soup.

Oh brother, Donna thinks. *Here we go.*

"My name is Special Agent Linwood F. Wilson," the FBI man says to Samir in a confident tone, flashing his badge. "Federal Bureau of Investigation." Samir nods. "This is Special Agent Ian A. Holm. We're looking into a crime that may be related to the murder of your employee, Mustapha Zizira." Samir nods again. "I need to ask you some questions." Another nod, but this time Samir delivers it after sucking on his fist and exhaling a prodigious smoke cloud that rolls like fog across the small tabletop and toward the FBI man. Donna wonders how he gets so much smoke from a single inhalation. It must have something to do with the way he holds the cigarette in the middle of his fist. Wilson looks at the smoke.

185

He does not like it, but Samir answers before the Fed can make up his mind as to whether it's a provocation.

"I help you. I want help you. I am proud American. Please, tell — how I help?"

"Well, I'll get right to the point," Wilson says, leaning in toward Samir. "Who killed Mustapha Zizira and why?" He holds a steady gaze on Samir, who returns his look for a short while, then breaks it to look at his older companion, then at Agent Holm, then at Detective Prima, then back at Agent Wilson. He raises both hands in bewildered surrender.

"This *your* job. You tell *me* who kill. I no know who kill."

Oops. It would have been okay to say "Beats me," Donna thinks. But it's not okay to tell the Man — "That's *your* job."

Wilson signals a nod at Holm, who takes out his badge and holds it shoulder high. His face suddenly bursts with hundreds of tiny sweat beads as he moves toward the seated diners.

"Ladies and gentlemen, I have to ask you all to step outside," he announces to everyone in the small restaurant. "FBI. Police action. Everybody out," he says. "This room is the scene of a police action. This way, please."

He moves among the four tables, holding his badge and making sweeping gestures with his arms as he directs the customers inside King Falafel to get up and exit, which they do — slowly, after looking back at the table where Wilson, Samir, and the other Syrian man watch with incredulity. Only the bedraggled man with the bushy grey hair remains seated.

This is going to be interesting, Donna thinks, knowing from the man's appearance that he's an indigenous Villager probably one step from full-blown vagrancy, dislikes cops, particularly dislikes Feds, and likely possesses zero modesty about expressing his opinions.

"Let's go," Holm says, towering over the man. "Outside."

Still holding his large soup spoon filled with rice pilaf and tomato sauce, the man slowly turns his head sideways. His face is leathery brown. His thin lips are coated with moist grains of white rice.

"I'm eating my breakfast," he says, speaking to the floor.

"Eat it outside," Holm retorts, tilting his thumb toward the door.

"You eat it outside," the man responds in a casual tone, his spoonful of pilaf still poised halfway to his mouth. "And while you're out there I believe you'll find plenty of dog shit on the curb to spread on your pita."

"That's enough. Either you exit this facility or I will exit you from this facility."

The man tilts his head up and examines the federal officer with disturbed eyes. "You certainly are fond of the word *facility.*"

"Let's go," Holm barks, shoving the man's shoulder. "Move or get moved. And don't think I'm worried about having to move you."

"Well, between the two of us, when it comes to worrying — you're the one sweating forty-five calibers."

"That's it. Let's go." Holm grabs the man by the elbow, which the man jerks away, sending the spoonful of rice and tomato sauce flying in an arc directly onto Agent Holm's light brown suit, white shirt, and brown necktie.

"Ha! Ya got pilaf on your Nazi uniform, ya brown-shirt bastard."

It is the last thing the man says. Holm easily hoists him by both shoulders, trots him to the door like he's an oversized string puppet, and deposits him into a standing position on the sidewalk. Holm closes the front door, the only door to King Falafel, and gestures to the cook to close the customer service window, which the cook does obediently. Donna suspects the cook is illegal; otherwise he would be less cooperative. Having a green card tends to embolden immigrants when it comes to cops.

Special Agent Ian A. Holm turns to stand guard in the entryway. He nods at Wilson.

"Right," says Wilson, turning to Samir. "Now, I'm going to ask you again. Who killed Mustapha Zizira and why?"

"Who . . . I . . . I no know," Samir sputters, wide-eyed and bewildered. "How I know?"

"We think you do know." Samir stares back at him. "What is your last name?"

"My last name bin-Assad."

"What is your full name?"

"My full, complete name Samir Ali bin Mohammed bin Yusef bin Assad."

"Have you ever been involved in any act of terror against the United States or any plan, effort, or plot to cause or bring about any act of terror in the United States or against the interests of the United States whether here or abroad?"

Samir's pupils dilate as he takes in the question. "No. I never."

"Was Mustapha Zizira involved in any act of terror against the United States or any plan, effort, or plot to cause or bring about

189

any act of terror in the United States or against the interests of the United States whether here or abroad?"

"No."

"How do you know?"

"I . . . well . . ."

"Yes?"

"I say no. I think no."

"Are you telling me you don't know for certain?"

"No, I not tell you. I tell you he come America — work. He got wife — beautiful. He got home — Queens. He no want hurt anybody."

"Have you ever been to Port Juttistown, New York?"

"Port what?"

"Port Juttistown."

"No. I never go. I never hear before of this place."

"Do you know a man named Hafez Oz Khalal?"

"No. Who this?"

"Are you any relation to Osama bin Laden?" Donna imagines she can see the ice glacier moving up Samir's neck, freezing his spine. He looks around the room, at his elderly companion, at Donna, and at Holm, who still stands guard in the doorway near the idle cook. Donna sees Samir's throat bobble as he swallows.

"I run King Falafel. My house — up. My work — down."

"Answer my question."

"No. I no relation. How could this be? He was Saudi. I am Syria."

"Well, you're both Muslim, you're both from the Middle East, and you both have a lot of 'bins' in your name." Samir blinks with astonishment. "Do you know a man named Hafez Oz Khalal, also known as Ozzy?"

"I say no already. Who this?"

Wilson stops interrogating. He stares coldly at the incredulous man. Donna knows it's an intentional pause, a strategy to heighten the man's insecurity about what is happening. Silence is nerve-wracking — especially for the guilty. The next one to speak is the loser. All Samir has to do is not talk, stop talking altogether. All he has to say is "Arrest me or go away; get a warrant or get lost." But he doesn't know that it really can be that easy. He's likely guessing that if he doesn't play along, the FBI will make his life very difficult in many ways — through city hall, the IRS, the board of health, harassing his suppliers with parking tickets, heck — even the phone company can suddenly be mystified about why his telephone doesn't work. He's right if that's what he's thinking. That stuff can easily happen.

Donna wonders what will come next. There aren't many options. Wilson can threaten the man with cop voodoo — stuff like arrest and deportation; or he can get nasty, or rather — nastier. That will probably not happen. Wilson is Velveeta on a stick, but he's not completely stupid. He doesn't want his name in the paper for the wrong reasons.

"All right. My partner and I are going to allow you to reopen your business," Wilson says, breaking the silence.

That's it, Donna thinks. Even though he doesn't realize it, Samir has just won because Wilson was the first to speak. "But we will remain in touch." Wilson stands and stares down with eyes that flash warning signs at the worried Syrian. "Very *close* touch," he says, striding away as though seeking escape from some foul odor.

Agent Holm opens the door and gestures for the cook to reopen the customer-service window as all three cops exit to the street, where only the rumpled man with bushy grey hair awaits them on the sidewalk. As they walk to the car, he follows behind, prancing like a court jester, regaling them with an oompah beer-hall ditty:

Hitler — he only had one ball.
Goering — had two but they were small.
Himmler — had something similar,
And Goebbels had no balls at all.
Dah . . . dat-dat-dat-dat-dat

He prances — raising his knees high and slapping his thighs rhythmically, as if they're bass drums. "Everybody now . . ."

Hitler — he only had one ball . . .

Donna nods with caution at the man as she passes him. *EDP,* she thinks — emotionally disturbed person. He's probably got records with both the NYPD and the psych ward on the 18th floor of Bellevue Hospital. Harmless enough, but never turn your back on an EDP, which both these Feds are doing right now, yet another indication that neither of them knows how to manage himself in the City.

She's made up her mind. The Q&A with Samir convinced her. There's stuff she wants to know. And in exchange for learning what she wants to learn, she'll swallow her pride and play along with these two clowns.

Well, a cop's gotta do what a cop's gotta do.

"Whew. All righty, then. Gentlemen, I apologize if I ever doubted you," she says from the back seat of the Ford Town Car. "Clearly you fellas are working something important . . . for the very highest authority . . . otherwise you wouldn't have . . . well, you know."

They glance back at her with the vaguest hint of an appreciative nod. It's not much, but it's enough to let Donna know it's working and worth choking down her professional dignity to continue.

"Listen, I know you fellas can't violate the whole 'your eyes only' thing. But let me help you. Tell me — what important fact did I omit from my report, and who is this Wizard of Ozzy man?"

The Feds exchange glances and she wonders if they're going to take the bait. She may have played it too heavy, laid it on too thick.

Come on, Tetris . . .

"The fact you omitted is . . . who killed Mustapha Zizira," Wilson says, looking back at her.

"Yeah. We really need to know that. That's why we had to lean on that guy," says Holm.

"Yeah. We can't risk that he's hiding something."

So far, so good.

"I'd like to know that too, gentlemen. Of course, I'd like to know only as a homicide cop. Obviously you guys want to know for other reasons." The two agents exchange the same knowing glance.

Come on, Tetris . . .

"Hafez Ozzy Khalal is an employee of Dutch Point," says Wilson. "Works in the containment structure."

"That's where the rods are," Holm explains. "Rods. As in nuclear rods. Nuclear. As in fissionable material. Fissionable, as in uranium."

"Oh my God!" Donna exclaims.

"Yeah. This is big," Wilson nods, raising his eyebrows. "If we've got to ruffle some A-rab feathers, that's just the way it is." He shrugs. "Hey, I think America is worth it."

"Well, we definitely need to find this Ozzy man," Donna says, encouraging them.

"Oh, we know where he is," says Wilson.

"Yeah," says Holm.

"You do?"

"Sure," they say in unison.

"Well, where?"

"At work. Up at Dutch Point." Wilson looks at his watch. "Right about now he'll be going on his meal break. He's on the early shift, starts work at 6 A.M. and brings his own breakfast. He's partial to cold fried eggs on pumpernickel."

"And hot tea," adds Agent Holm, "sweetened with honey."

Donna decides to test them for reaction, but without actually asking a question.

Keep going, Tetris . . .

"Well, if you know what he's toting in his lunchbox when he goes to work, I just hope he's not toting out a thermos full of uranium in the same lunchbox when he leaves work."

Again, Wilson and Holm exchange glances, but this time they are glances of discomfort. They are on the verge of ceasing all conversation and she needs to recover — fast. "Jesus, how did a Syrian terrorist ever get a job working around nukes? Somebody at Immigration must have been busted back to file clerk."

"Nah. He came over 17 years ago on a student visa," says Wilson. "Got a Ph.D. in nuclear physics from the University of Minnesota. Got naturalized. Never went abroad again. That stuff all washes clean."

Keep going, Tetris . . .

"Oh. Well, that's good anyway," Donna says with feigned relief.

But wait. Something else just sparked.

Minnesota. What's so interesting about Minnesota? To her — nothing. Nothing could be more *UN*-interesting than Minnesota.

"Gentlemen, I can't stifle my curiosity any longer. What's this Ozzy's connection to our dead man Zizira or our man Samir in King Falafel who's still trembling in his nightgown after you guys worked him over?"

Keep going, Tetris . . .

"Nothing major," says Wilson. "We found the phone number of that wog-shop in Hafez Ozzy Khalal's cell phone directory. Maybe it's something, maybe it's nothing. Maybe he just likes the slop they make in there. But when we learned there had been a murder here last year, it turned into a more interesting phone number."

"Either way, we had to check it out," shrugs Holm. "You know, they all stick together. Islam is the glue for these people. American citizen or not . . . Minnesota or not . . ." He pauses, shrugs, smirks. "It doesn't matter to them."

So, these two are only on a fishing trip. That's all they're doing. They're trolling, trying to flush a Greenwich Village flounder by banging pots and pans in the water. The Tetris pieces are falling *kah-chunk* very nicely.

The EDP is still prancing near the car, still singing his oompah ditty. Wilson and Holm seem amused by him. They wouldn't be so amused if he'd cracked a table over their heads when they turned their backs on him.

So what have they got? They've got one guy, male, Syrian-American with a big-ticket science job suspected of stealing something from a nuke plant that may mean the end of the United States as we know it, and his cell phone directory has King Falafel's number programmed in it.

"Is that true?" Wilson asks his partner.

"What?"

"That Hitler only had one ball."

Holm chuckles. "Yeah, I think so. Just imagine if he'd had two."

"Hmm," says Wilson, "we'd probably be sprechenden Deutsch right now."

It's the first time Donna has heard either of them laugh. And they're not only laughing, but loudly guffawing like a couple of frat boys, which makes her smile too. Well, in all fairness, it *was* amusing.

She mulls the situation. Nothing she'd seen or heard changes Donna's original instinctive guess that case H-7211 was an execution by an acquaintance with a vendetta. Of course, it could have been an acquaintance related somehow to Ozzy. That would be bad, especially if it meant the end of the world. But Samir's reaction was solid. He handled his FBI shakedown very well. Nothing he did or said seemed phony, convincing her that he really knows nothing. For him, life really is a matter of "my family — up, my work — down." If Zizira was working on a terror thing, then Samir really didn't know anything about it.

The Feds grow bored watching the EDP. Holm cranks the engine on the Ford Town Car.

"Listen, Detective Prima," Wilson says. "We've got to go upstate for the balance of the afternoon. Check on some stuff up there. But we'll be back. If not tomorrow, certainly later in the week. We need to talk to your dead man's widow in Queens. Maybe you can help grease our path on that. We'll probably go easy on her, at least for the first visit."

Things are looking up. Special Agent Linwood F. Wilson just called her "Detective." That's a first. Kissing up to the guy is all it took for a fast turnaround.

"Yeah," says Holm. "And I know we don't have to say it. But we have to say it. All that stuff we were talking about is strictly confidential. I mean, *ultra* confidential. We may be close to finding . . . or, uh, figuring this thing out."

"Can we drop you anywhere?" Wilson asks.

"I'll get out here. The Sixth is a short walk. I like walking. Listen, you guys, good luck. Pull me back in this week whenever you need me."

"Will do."

Before Donna opens the car door, she asks, "I was just wondering, what's the town in Minnesota where your man went to college?"

"Duluth."

"Never heard of it," Donna says, stepping to the sidewalk on Leroy Street.

2
King Falafel — Part II

Detective Donna Prima readies her cop voice.

"Shut up or get locked up," she barks at the EDP, who immediately halts his irritating oompah song and stops prancing. She leers at two falafel customers sitting on the nearby bench who've been amusing themselves by quietly singing along with him as back-up chorus. They stop singing and look away, as though she is suddenly invisible.

"This city owes me breakfast," the EDP demands, standing his ground, arms akimbo, snapping his head and throwing back his bushy grey hair.

Donna waits for the Town Car to fully turn the corner at Bleecker Street before approaching King Falafel. Samir is standing at the door, set to burst with nervous agitation.

"Samir, I want to buy this guy a refill on his order. Make it to go."

Samir nods, gestures rapidly to the cook in the window, and speaks a round of fast instructions in Arabic as he points behind the counter at a series of aluminum trays in the small front kitchen space. Fifteen seconds later the cook hands the EDP a bag containing a tinfoil dish filled with rice pilaf, garnished with hot peppers, a heaping spoon of hummus, two balls of falafel, two steaming pieces of pita toast coated with garlic butter, plastic fork, knife, napkins, and a takeout menu.

"There. Now you've got your two balls, Mr. Song-and-Dance man. Now get out of here," she barks. "And don't plan on getting booked on *American Idol* anytime soon."

The EDP snorts, takes the bag, and scurries away without further complaint. Donna watches to make certain he really departs, then gestures to withdraw money, but Samir waves her off.

"No money for this." He sighs, shrugs, and raises his hands, palms up. "What I do?" he asks, his eyes turning moist. "What I do?"

"You didn't do anything. Listen Samir, I can't say too much, okay? Those guys have got to do what they have got to do. I just want you to understand that."

"I tell you. I tell them. I tell everybody. I

just want work. I no know nothing. I just know my family — up. My work — down."

"Samir, I'm trying to tell you something important."

"What? I bring my family America. My three little girls. What I do?"

She leans into the roly-poly man wearing a flowing seersucker toga and orange flip-flops.

"Samir, take a breath!"

He finally settles down, leaning onto the takeout counter, his forehead in both hands.

"Okay, Capp-itahn. You tell me. What?"

"Number one: you did nothing wrong. Number two: you have nothing to worry about. Those two are finished with you. That's it."

"They no be back?" he sniffles, raising his head.

"No."

She stands with Samir and the cook in the King Falafel entryway for a short while. She can't be certain that Wilson and Holm will not return. But it's unlikely they will. And whether they do or not, it's clear they've got nothing, so why not do the right thing for this guy? Make him rest a little easier. Of course, it's that sort of thing that got her in trouble with Captain Hurly and taken off homicide for six months, but this seems harmless enough.

"Okay, Capp-itahn. Thank you for coming back. You want lunch?" He gestures behind the counter at the array of falafel, hummus, baba ganoush, and the giant spit of shawarma rotating in the vertical rotisserie perched in the window. The idea is disgusting to her. It all looks so mushy, like multicolored barf.

"No, thank you, Samir, I've got to go. But let me ask you a question. Do you remember where Mustapha Zizira's wife was from — originally?"

"Her parent Syria."

"No, I mean where was she born?"

"Oh, she born America."

"But do you remember where exactly?"

He pauses to think, looks down at the floor as he pulls at his lips with wide fat fingers.

"Eh!" he barks, his face glowing with pride. "I remember."

"Okay?"

"Duluth, Minnesota."

Kah-chunk goes Tetris.

3
QUIET ON THE SET

The she-vampires swarm around the giant round bed and the large French window open from floor to ceiling. Their chiffon nighties blow with a fake breeze created by two men standing just off camera, each waving a large board of foam core. The pale zaftig girls with colorful eyeshadow have cat pupils. Donna can barely see the harness suspending the two who levitate — *those* two wear opaque nighties and what looks like leotards underneath. The others wear gauzy chiffon that, as Aunt Mary would say, "puts all their bibs and bobs on full display."

"Lights!" a voice calls out. The lights dim in the bedroom as they glow hotter outside the French window. "Stand by, harness crew. Fog machine. Okay. Red lights. Okay. Let's see that moon. Great. And . . . first vampire . . . Branden . . . come on down."

A he-vampire glides down outside the window, then through the window, then alights on the floor as the she-vampires hiss and snarl in fang-baring delight.

How do they do that? Donna wonders. *How do they make that guy glide?*

"Good! Okay, next two vampires . . . Mikhail and Crawford . . . come on down . . . good."

They too glide down and through the window and — look at that, one of them is Conner Anderson. These two are also swarmed by the she-vampires.

"Great! Okay, Sasha and Penderliz, you two gradually lead Branden to the bed. That's it. Now the rest of you girls, escort Mikhail and Crawford to the bed. Great. Keep it up . . . keep it up . . . lots of fang . . . everybody gimme more fang . . . *more fang* . . . great . . . lots of kissing now . . . . let's get more fog in here . . . okay, Sasha, you feel Branden's body all over while Penderliz, you just concentrate on kissing Branden . . . great . . . gimme a wide shot of the whole room . . . now gradually tighten that down . . . tighter . . . tighter . . . tighter . . . you're aiming for Branden's mouth . . . tighter . . . great . . . gimme a tight close-up on that mouth . . . keep kissing . . . and . . . cut!"

The studio becomes an instant swarm of stagehands rolling away walls that snap apart at the seams. The harnesses that held the floating vampires are unhitched and left dangling below a grid of iron bars where hundreds of tubular Leko lights hang.

"What a load of crap," Donna announces with laughter when Conner joins her in the small audience area rising up from the set.

"Shh. Not so loud," he says. "We take this stuff very seriously. Actor egos and all that."

"Yeah, I bet. Which one are you, Mikhail or Crawford?"

"Crawford."

"Figures. You don't look much like a Mikhail. How do they make you fly through the window like that?"

"Double pullies. Very expensive."

"What about that guy barking instructions? Won't that mess it up?"

"No. They'll dub music over that — organ, timpani, chanting monks, all that spooky stuff. That scene was the closer for the week. It caps a subplot about the boy vamps proving to the girl vamps that we can seduce the living just as well as they can. We just flew back from a gala at the Metropolitan Museum, where we attacked everybody, sucking blood until it ran through the French Impressionist wing, through the Rembrandt room, down the main staircase, out the doors, and down Fifth Avenue."

"So, what now?" Donna asks.

"I'm done. I finished my dialogue shots for the week, so I'm free and clear for the night and all day tomorrow. How about some dinner?"

"Sounds good. But I feel like walking a little. That okay with you?"

"Sure. As long as we don't get run over."

They walk to the corridor, where Donna suggests they take the stairs down to the plaza level instead of the elevator. Outside, they walk around the skating rink to Sixth Avenue, where tourists line up to buy tickets at Radio City Music Hall. The marquee advertises a charity blood-drive concert. Buy a ticket now, walk around the corner to give blood, get your ticket stamped at the blood center, and come back tonight and hear a bunch of celebrities, including Tony Bennett.

"I bet you like Tony Bennett," Conner says.

"That would be correct."

"You want to buy tickets? Give blood? Come back tonight?"

Donna considers it. It's certainly appropriate. Her work is routinely about people who lose their blood and others who spill it. Now she's growing more and more fond of a vampire from Dixie who makes a living sucking it.

"Nah, we've got more important stuff to do. Like catching up on lost time."

"I hope this work does not include becoming roadkill." Conner speaks with quiet honesty as they cross Sixth Avenue.

Looking down at the pavement, Donna nods in agreement. The grisly attempt on their lives two days earlier is still a jarring ugliness for them both. It was so horrible — all they could do was lie next to each other in the bed at the Angel Motel in Lapa, Pennsylvania — fully clothed, staring at the whirring fan in the ceiling, talking little as morning turned into afternoon. They were both very grateful to be alive — even if it meant not having sex, which is exactly what it meant.

"You okay?" he had said with uncertainty, lying next to her.

"Uh . . . yeah. You?"

"I think so," he'd said. That was about all they could manage as they recovered from the shock of coming face to face with their mortality. They repeated the exchange several times for the two hours they lay there — paralyzed with dread, and Donna's mind racing as she ruminated on the puzzle that suddenly grew more puzzling with attempted murder. Or was it really attempted murder? Accidents do happen. Maybe the idiot driving that trash truck was text-messaging. Esther did say the truckers don't talk on their cell phones because they can't hear anything, so they probably text. Neither of them saw the driver. They were both too thoroughly absorbed with watching the front of the truck, the biplane hood orna-ment, and the swerving tires, which all hap-pened, as they say — so fast. They couldn't know if it was Motty in his white fur coat, Joe Fibonacci with his sculpted flattop, or some other thug. On the drive back to the City, she'd been so occupied with the details of the case (which may not even *be* a case) that she'd almost forgotten about her claus-trophobia.

From Sixth Avenue they walk a casual zigzag to Times Square, where the crowd of tourists grows to a tidal wave of humanity. Unlike the rest of New York City's popula-tion, the vast majority here appears plain, innocent, and unassuming. For Donna, their looks peg them all as being from — out there. They are pilgrims to the greatest city the world has ever known, the one city where a strike by some gang of holy-rolling yahoos did more than spill blood — it also chalked up a score in the category of sym-bolic victory. For them, 9/11 was really just one big "gotcha!"

But what if Agents Wilson and Holm are actually onto something? Numbskulls or not, they could be onto some really big plot, some bone-chilling, blood-spilling design being mapped out to put the yahoos on the big board a second time with even more splash than the first. If so, *this* would be the place, she thinks — Times Square — the center of the city, the capital of the whole cocky non-Muslim world. It's already happened once. Thank goodness that guy turned out to be more of a Blockhead Bomber than the real deal. Not only did his bomb fizzle, but he locked the keys of his getaway car inside the bomb car. That was pure luck for the police. *Next time around . . . well, let's not think about it.*

But hold up there. It's difficult for her to imagine that those two J. Edgar wannabes could possibly be onto anything worthwhile — and certainly not anything *really* worthwhile, not like 007-saves-the-world worthwhile. The *very highest authority* wouldn't entrust those two with stuff that important, would it?

Donna's rumination is halted when Conner stops in the middle of Times Square, directly under the statue of George M. Cohan. When Conner looks into her eyes, she knows what he's thinking and can guess what he's about to suggest.

"Hey, Pink Pistol Lady, I've got an idea. Let's go back to my place. We can have pasta and wine at Napoli Ristorante. Then we can go upstairs. It's pretty messy. I'm packing up for my move. But if you're still interested . . ." He smiles seductively.

Donna takes a deep breath as she scans the crowd of angelic American pilgrims crowding Times Square. She turns to give him the same willing smile she gave him Friday afternoon in his apartment to let him know she's interested.

"You know something, Vampire Man, that sounds pretty fine to me. Let's go."

4
A LITTLE BIT OF THIS —
A LITTLE BIT OF THAT

They sit at a window table that looks out on Eighth Avenue, the liquor store, and O'Toole's Bar on the opposite side of the street. Nothing seems unusual. Pedestrian traffic is much slower on a Monday night, with far fewer customers coming and going from both businesses.

Donna contemplates asking the waiter about the Mob hit that took place during the glory days, but changes her mind. The History Channel should do a program on The Top Ten Mob Hits Nobody Remembers. She would watch it.

Conner and Donna share a large salad and a small carafe of red wine. They order individual bowls of pasta. They talk little. He's still recovering from learning that playing boy detective can get you killed. She's still obsessed with thoughts about nearly getting squished like a bug, Agents Wilson and Holm, the crowd of innocent Americans in the Times Square Mecca, 9/11, and her father's advice to rely on her instincts. It's not unlike a game of Tetris, where she manipulates the button, making the geometric shapes spin around, turn this way, then that way, then upside-down as she tries to fit them all together into a cohesive whole and make everything go *kah-chunk*.

"Great spaghetti Bolognese," Conner mumbles with a mouthful of loose ends dangling past his lips.

"The fettucini Alfredo is good too," Donna grunts, sopping a piece of bread in the butter sauce.

Actually, Donna thinks, working these three separate crimes and watching the details chug forward is a lot like the real Tetris. And they have three levels of seriousness: one may involve potential national calamity, another is a gang of lowlife counterfeiters or druggies, and the third is a common break-and-enter job committed by a lone Russian skuzzo with a pull-and-pry bar. The irony is, she's not authorized to be working *any* of them — let alone working all of them with a Southern civilian soap-opera actor who, it must be admitted, she appears to be growing more fond of by the minute.

"I've made a decision," she announces.

"Me too," Conner responds. "I've decided I have to dine in this place more frequently. What's your decision?"

"Nothing quite as important. Just this." She ticks off elements of her plan, one per finger. "First, I have to get inside the common cellar over there. Second — I have do it without being caught and murdered in the process. Third — depending on what I see, we may have to go back to Port Jujube tonight for another round of trash talk. Only this time, four — we have to go secretly by way of the back door of that giant dump, wherever the back door is, and five — we have to do it without *you* being caught and murdered in the process or eaten alive by some junkyard dog, because that would get me in more trouble than I can handle."

Conner's cheeks slowly puff outward. "Whew," he exhales.

"Are you with me?" she asks.

Conner nods with exasperation and takes care of the check. Back in apartment 4, overlooking O'Toole's Bar and the liquor store, Donna goes to work.

"You've got a land line telephone, right?"

"Yeah. By the couch."

"You listed in the book?"

"Not anymore. I had to change my number and go unlisted once I started work on the soap."

"Too much jailbait wanting to come visit?"

"You don't miss much, do you?"

"Not as a rule."

Donna sits and dials the number in Los Angeles, Pennsylvania. Wilson and Holm said he works the early shift, so unless he's doing some late shopping at Walmart, he ought to be in bed by now.

"Hello?"

"Hello, I'm trying to reach Hafez Khalal."

"This is Hafez Khalal."

"Hello, Mr. Khalal. I'm conducting a survey about food preferences. Do you have a few moments, sir?"

"How did you get my name and number?"

"From the phone book. We're looking for opinions of people with a taste for ethnic foods. You know — immigrants."

"My listing only identifies me as H. Khalal. And I am not an immigrant. I am an American citizen."

"Oh, sorry, sir. We usually get all names and numbers from the phone book. Sometimes they come from other sources like magazine subscriptions. Anyway, we're looking for your opinions on a very important subject pertaining to Arab-Americans. It's all about food. Perhaps you would agree, Mr. Khalal, there's very little in life as important as food. Do you have a few moments, sir?"

The pause is more than a pause. It is the type of silence heard in the cemetery at midnight. Donna imagines she can hear the churning wheels of self-preservation in the brain of this nuclear engineer. She remembers the TV director shouting things like "more fang, let me see more fang." Ha. *More churning wheels,* she thinks. *Louder. Let me hear the wheels of your fancy American-Minnesota education churning in my ear. Let's hear those neurons of fear popping like the Fourth of July, Mr. Khalal!*

"What company?" he finally asks in a slow monotone.

"I'm calling on behalf of the Leroy Food Company based in Duluth, Minnesota. We're the biggest manufacturer of ethnic frozen foods in the U.S. and we're calling today with a survey about whether you may be interested in a new brand of frozen falafel that will soon find its way to the frozen-food section of your local supermarket. If you have a just a few minutes I'd like to ask you some questions about . . ."

Click goes the phone line.

Kah-chunk go all the geometric shapes on the Tetris screen.

Let Mr. Khalal worry about that for a

while. If her guess is right, he got the phone number from Caller ID. If he's smart, and she guesses that nuclear engineers tend to be smarter than the average Joe, he'll try to look up the number in the reverse directory. When he finds nothing listed, it'll make him worry even more. At some point — he'll call back. Maybe when he does, he'll have something interesting to say. If he doesn't call back, if he panics and runs, he'll get picked up by Dufus and Dorkus — the FBI men who answer only to the *very highest authority.* If that happens, she'll clue in Detective Sporietto when he returns from vacation, so that while the FBI works their terror case, the NYPD goes to work on a one-year-old murder case. Either way, she wins.

There is just one little problem: she could be wrong. What if he really is a holy-rolling yahoo for Allah? If that's the case, she may have just hastened along a plot to do a jihad number on thousands of tourists in Times Square. But like her dad advised, she has to rely on her instincts.

In this case, her instincts have a whole laundry list. She ticks them off. First — the Zizira murder had a non-terror motive. Second — if there was terror involved, Samir would know something; nothing goes on in that falafel joint that he doesn't know about, and she is convinced he's being honest when he says he knows nothing. Third — the FBI couldn't locate a loud Italian fart in a Mexican bean factory. They missed it on 9/11. What makes anyone think they know what they're doing this time around? For her the answer is: nothing.

"What'd that guy do?" Conner asks, interrupting her effort to rationalize what she's just done.

"That's what I'm trying to find out."

"So you pose as a frozen-food surveyor from Duluth?"

"Never mind," she barks, instantly annoyed at his sarcasm. "It's not *our* case. *Our* case is the one outside that window. How about you focus on that one? Do me a favor, turn off your answering machine. If this guy calls back, just hand the phone to me."

"How will I know it's him?"

"Do you normally get calls from paranoid Arabs who want to know who you are?"

"Can't say that I do."

"Well, if you do — that'll be him."

She sits at the foot of the bed under Laurence Olivier emoting over the skull of Yorick and peeks through the maroon venetian blinds. Outside, noisy traffic flows past in relative order, controlled by the traffic light directly below. The streetlights are already on, casting a yellow arc over everything. The distant strains of "Honky Tonk Women" can be heard playing on the jukebox in the back of O'Toole's.

The fact that business is slower now on Monday night will only make it more difficult to get into the cellar, because the cashier in the liquor store and the bartender in O'Toole's Bar will be less distracted. She flips open her cell phone and dials.

"Lo . . . O'Toole's," comes the answer. The music is blasting so loudly Donna can barely hear over Mick Jagger's belting "gimme, gimme, gimme, blah-blah, blah-blah blues."

"Is Billy in tonight?"

"Can't hear. Speak up."

Donna takes a deep breath. "IS BILLY TENDING BAR?" she shouts into the cell phone.

"NO! BILLY'S OFF MONDAY."

"THANKS. GOODBYE."

Well, at least that's one break. With Billy Average, the Mean Bartender, out of the way, she won't be recognized. It'll be easier to get into the cellar through the bar. Having seen the back room of the liquor store, she knows there's no visible trap door there, so it's either very well concealed in the back room, or it's in the floor behind the main sales counter. Either way, it's going to be difficult to convince the clerk in the liquor store to step aside while she goes poking around behind the cash register. Of course, she needs to have a Plan B if that metal door near the toilet in the bar is bolted shut, which it probably is because it's Monday. She knows from experience that dopers generally take Monday off. Look at Billy the Mean Bartender — he's off today. But it's still a chance worth taking.

"You programmed the number for O'Toole's Bar into your cell?" Conner asks.

"Yep. Why?"

"Nothing," he shrugs. "It's kind of impressive that you think ahead like that."

BR-RING-G-G.

"Speaking of phones. That's your land line," she says. "I'll get it."

She goes back to the small living room and sits on the couch.

"Hello, King Polling Company, how may I help you?" Silence follows. Background traffic noise tells Donna that Khalal's calling from a pay phone.

"Is anyone there? This is King Polling Company." More silence. "Ahem, are you calling to take a survey?"

"You phoned me," the voice says, breaking the silence. Donna can barely hear the hint of a Middle Eastern accent in the voice, which sounds deep and intelligent.

"All right, sir. Do you know the subject of the survey I phoned you about? Was it a political survey about the upcoming November elections? Was it about frozen food for the Leroy Company? Or was it the survey about your opinions on U.S. national security?" After another long silence, the voice speaks again.

"What do you want?" it asks. This time it's Donna's turn to pause. She holds the silence for a protracted time and suddenly speaks as though there has been no pause at all.

"This is King Polling Company, sir. Do you know the subject of the survey you were phoned about?"

Click.

"Perfect," Donna shouts, delighted with the result. "He'll be sweating that the rest of the night. Maybe even the rest of the week."

"For somebody not allowed to do case work — you certainly have a lot of cases," Conner says from the bed in the adjacent room. "What do we do now?"

"First, get your cell phone and program my number on your auto-call. Second, sit down on the bed and keep your eyes open. Third, I'm going back to O'Toole's, only this time I'm going by myself while you watch from the window and keep a phone connection with me, letting me know anything important."

"Just like the lowlifes who jacked my apartment . . ."

"Exactly."

". . . who you are working hard to catch so they can be guillotined in Times Square by the mayor, which is the only reason why I am helping you."

"Right," Donna barks in full cop voice. "One crime at a time!"

5
WHAT A LOSER

"Budweiser."

Donna takes one of the many vacant stools in O'Toole's Bar. The juke is playing "Louie Louie," the TV is tuned to wrestling, and the bartender is an older man, tall, with an unruly clump of wavy brown hair mixed with bright streaks of whitish-grey. He has a nimble sort of world-weary manner about him. Her bristling radar tells her at first sight that he's a "friendly." If he were a "hostile," she would know that too, but there's something else about this guy.

"Thanks," she says chugging half the bottle and wiping her mouth. "You wouldn't be Mr. O'Toole, would you?"

"Nah, I'm Jimmy Dougheney, the other owner. Well, now I'm the only owner. Tom O'Toole passed away a couple o' years back. Heart attack."

"Oh, I'm sorry to hear it."

"Yeah," Jimmy shrugs. "Tom was a good

fella. But you know, when your number's up . . ." He shrugs again, bigger this time. "I just work Mondays, just to keep my hand in. You know."

"I hear ya," she says sympathetically. "Hey, how come you didn't name it 'Tom & Jimmy's Bar,' or 'TJ's,' or something like that?"

"Oh, we were cops. Partners. Tom got shot. He recovered and opened this place by himself. I bought in after I retired."

Kah-chunk.

Her instincts were dead on. Tom and Jimmy ran this mostly Irish cop bar for the past 25 years or so. When he says "partner," he means partner in the squad car *and* partner in business.

"Well, letting nature take ya with a heart attack is better than getting a nameplate on the wall of honor down at One Police Plaza."

"How'd you know about that?"

"I saw it on a school trip in the seventh grade," Donna says, recovering quickly from her misstep and avoiding the question he's likely to ask, which is the universal question one cop asks to identify another: "Are you on the job?"

"We even got to see a demonstration in the shooting gallery," Donna adds, telling a true story that sparked her first thoughts of becoming a cop. She drains the balance of her beer in one long chug. "Hit me again, Jimmy."

"You got all these fancy gizmos today," Jimmy says, nodding at her ear while uncapping another bottle. "My oldest kid is a lawyer. He walks around all day with a thing just like that stuck in his ear. What's it called?"

"Bluetooth headset."

"Yeah, that's it. When it's not Bluetooth, it's the iPods, or the Blackberries, or iBerries or PodBerries or some such thing. I have enough trouble telling real berries from grapes. I can't keep any of these gadgets straight."

"I agree, Jimmy. I get overloaded too. My dad says the fountain pen was around for a thousand years before the ballpoint got invented. That's enough time to get used to a thing before it's improved upon. But now — everything happens too fast." Jimmy nods with waning interest. Donna turns her second beer bottle up and takes a long swallow, gurgling loudly as the beer flows down her throat.

"You're drinking too fast."

"Excuse me?"

"Say what?" Jimmy the Nice Bartender asks.

"Nothing, I must be hearing things." Donna realizes the admonishment against drinking too fast did not come from Jimmy the Nice Bartender but rather from Conner Anderson — the voice inside her ear.

"Don't get drunk," the voice says. "Remember you had wine too."

A moment later a man emerges from the back of the bar, still zipping up his fly. Donna intuitively knows that he's going to take a shot at her. She absorbs his description: male-white, 5'8," 190 pounds with a full-blown beer belly so swollen it looks nine months pregnant, pit-bull face . . . and a shaved head.

He gives Donna a prolonged stare, but first goes to the jukebox, where "Louie Louie" has concluded. He slips more quarters into the slot, pushing buttons for "Jumpin' Jack Flash" and "Wild Thing." He retrieves his beer bottle from the end of the bar near the toilet and relocates to the available stool next to Donna, where he introduces himself as Jake and immediately complains that the juke does not have any selections by his favorite group, Grand Funk Railroad.

"Never heard of 'em," says Donna, thinking it to be the worst opening line she's ever heard. Her response is all the introduction he needs to launch into an odd, rambling monologue about himself and the principal complaints of his life: first, the poorly-performing Yankees; second, no smoking in bars; and third, the new bicycle lanes on the city's main avenues, which he prophesies to be the end of the world as we know it.

"Shake this loser," says the voice inside Donna's ear.

"I'm with you," Donna says, pretending agreement. "This city was not designed for bicyclists."

"Damn right," Jake rejoins with enthusiasm. "Let 'em all go to Beijing. Let 'em ride their wheelchairs on that Ho Chi Minh Highway or whatever that thing is called. Either that, or get a real bike. You know — a Harley, unless Mayor Mike creates a special day for squishin'. If he would do that — they can stick around."

"Squishing?"

"Yeah. You know." He holds a long look at her with a proud twinkle in his pit-bull eyes as he turns up his Budweiser bottle for a generous chug, his naked head shining in the dark bar. She waits for his bottle to fall away from his mouth before responding.

"Not really. What's squishing?"

"Well, it's like — they got 'Take Your Daughter to Work Day.' Right?"

"Right."

"And they got 'Stop Smoking Day.' Right?"

"Right."

"So, if the mayor created 'Squish a Bicyclist Day' — then for one day every year we could ride around and smash 'em without worrying about getting a ticket or nothing. Man, that would be great." His eyes twinkle with anticipation.

The disembodied voice crackles in her ear. "I give you my permission to pull your little pink gun and blast this maniac right now."

"It could even be the start of other good stuff," Jake continues.

"Please don't ask him," the voice says.

"Like what?" Donna asks, pretending to be interested.

"Well, you know, like we could have 'Bag a Fag Day.' Or, if you're allowed to run over 'em — we could call it 'Smear a Queer Day.' " He makes a saluting gesture, tipping his shaved head and snapping his hand in the air in respect of the idea. "Now *that* would help make this city great again — great like it used to be when men were men and pansies were pansies."

"This guy reminds me of why I don't miss Tupelo," Conner says.

"Another beer?"

"Sure, Jimmy. That would be great." Donna accepts her third beer and takes a small sip. "Well, that's an interesting civic-minded wish list you have there, Jake. Good luck convincing City Hall." His hard brown eyes wonder if she's agreeing with him or getting snotty, but she stops him thinking before he can make a decision. "Listen, this lady needs to visit the little girls' room. Watch my beer for me, will ya?"

Jake gives an inebriated nod in the affirmative as the juke begins playing "Wild Thing" by The Troggs. He hammers his head in the air along with the hammering of the iconic guitar lick: *dah-dah . . . da-da-dum-dum-DAH-DAH.*

Unlike Billy Average the Mean Bartender, Jimmy the Nice Bartender takes no notice of her as she walks the length of the bar to the small back corridor. The flimsy toilet door is locked. Good. That'll be a good excuse for her absence from the bar for longer than a routine pee would require. Now for the other door, the gateway to the secret of this joint — whatever that secret may be.

Locked! Blast.

"Listen, Vampire Man, the door is bolted," Donna whispers into her headset. "I'm going back to the bar. Let's go into a holding pattern and hope that something develops."

"Yes, let's do," says Conner's voice in her ear. "Otherwise Mr. Homicidal Homophobe is going to turn you into a trophy and hang you on his wall."

"I can handle him. I'm a cop, remember?"

"Wow. We better call Guinness," Jake announces when she returns. "I think we could get you listed as the quickest sit-down pee'er on record."

"Very funny. The door was locked. I guess some guy is in there."

Jake quickly refocuses on himself and launches into a second round of mindless complaints about the ways of the world — this time enumerating a list that includes Arabs, guys with ponytails and hip-hoppers (whom he calls hippity-hoppities) who wear the waistline of their blue jeans around the middle of their ass. As for preferences, those ways of the world for which he holds a raconteur's fine liking — the list includes Ireland, Ford's F-line series of pickup trucks, Harleys, Budweiser, men who actually work for a living such as welders and auto-body repairmen and — as he puts it, "women who pack an 8-cylinder SUV in the back of their britches."

Donna notices that whenever he concentrates or puts emphasis on certain words to let her know he really means it, to make it clear that he's really, really serious — there appears on his upper forehead a little triangular fleshy mass, just above where the hairline would be if he had any hair. It appears out of nowhere, a doughy lump that holds its swollen three-sided outline until the intensity of his declamation eases, which makes it disappear completely.

She lets Jake drone on, tuning out most of what he says during her stakeout of the bar's inner sanctum, occasionally watching the triangular little tumor that rises and falls on Jake's forehead. If this creepoid were a robot, that thing would be a microchip, she decides, some computerized hard drive that controls everything he says and does.

While slowly nursing her third beer, Donna becomes aware that Conner hasn't whispered any of his smarty-pants remarks into her headset for a while. She interrupts Jake's unending monologue.

"Excuse me, Jake. I'm gonna try that powder room thing again." The triangle on his head disappears while she speaks, but reappears as he responds with an earnest nod. In the back corridor she checks the metal door. Still bolted shut. She leans into the corner that allows the most privacy and whispers into the headset.

"Hey, Vampire Man. You still with me?"

"I'm here," says Conner. "I made coffee. Would you like some?"

"No thanks."

"You keep drinking and you're going to need some."

"I don't need it. I'm on the job. And don't be lingering in the kitchen making coffee when you should be watching my back."

"Okay, okay. I am watching. There's nothing new. But I'm tired of listening to that loser hit on you. He reminds me of Uncle Sammy's son, Cousin Earl, who used to call me things like Conner the Cutie and Andy the Dandy."

Maybe he's right, she decides. Things are not going well. It may be better to throw in the towel for the night, return to the vampire's nest. It's actually not a bad idea. But before she can speak Conner's voice bursts with excitement over the Bluetooth.

"Hey, Sherlock. The game's afoot — white Rolls Royce. Directly out front."

"Okay. Keep me posted," she says, racing back to the barstool.

"It's what's his name, Joe Fibonacci," Conner says in her ear. "Just him, nobody else. Hey, he must be a weightlifter, he's busting with muscles that I didn't notice the other night. He's not going into the bar.

He's going into the liquor store."

"Hey Jimmy, let me settle up," Donna tells the nice bartender. Jake waves her off.

"I've got your beers," he says, pushing a wad of fives and singles across the countertop toward the bartender, who selects only enough money to pay for Donna's Budweisers.

Conner continues his narration: "Okay, he's walking past the clerk in the liquor store like he owns the place. I've lost sight of him now, but I don't think he's shopping for Chardonnay."

"Thanks," Donna says.

"You're welcome," comes the response in stereo, one from Jake sitting on the barstool to her left, the other from Conner speaking in her right ear. Donna leans into her third beer. Despite having consumed half a carafe of wine and two full Budweisers, she is suddenly perfectly sober after tilting toward tipsy. Funny how that works. She wonders if it's some adrenaline thing, some message the brain delivers to the blood and liver to quit feeling sloshed because the owner of the body may need it for doing something other than feeling happily tight. She recalls Conner's tale about the antelope who stomped a lion, all because of the power of adrenaline.

Jake's cell phone goes off with a ringtone song. "Ah, 'Big Buns' by Grand Funk," he says proudly. "My favorite band." He answers the call, listens for two seconds as the triangular mass appears on his forehead, says "Okay," folds the phone, and replaces it in his pocket. He eyes Jimmy suspiciously, making the triangle even more distinct, but the nice bartender with the brightly streaked hair is paying little attention to anything except the wrestling match on TV.

Jake spins his pregnant belly toward Donna.

"Okay, Miss Quick Pee'er, my boss is having my truck bought around, so I gotta head out for a little while. Maybe you'll be here when I get back."

"Sounds like a plan," Donna says as Jake hurries from his barstool.

Donna's radar is vibrating, but she's uncertain why. She strains to look at the street but observes nothing remarkable. She can see the distinctive rear end of the Rolls where it's parked in front of the liquor store, and she wonders why Joe Fibonacci would not enter the bar like he did Friday night. And why would Jake suddenly be worried about Jimmy the Nice Bartender which, based on his bulging triangle, he clearly was?

"Okay," says Conner's voice, "we've got a

new customer going into the liquor store, a bald-headed man with a huge beer belly. I don't know if you saw him, but he just came out of the bar where you are, turned right, and hustled into the liquor store."

Madre di Dio — Jake! He got the call and went next door to hook up with the boss.

"Okay," Conner says, "Bald man just waltzed past the liquor store clerk and disappeared in the back like Fibonacci did a minute ago."

Donna quickly considers running after Jake on the pretense that she's interested in him and wants to pop the question — My place or yours? — and accidentally on purpose catch them both red-handed doing whatever it is they're doing: dope, murder, printing up counterfeit Benjamins. But she decides to wait. Whatever they're doing — they're not going to stop doing it tonight.

"Hey Jimmy, what do you know about that guy?"

"Who, Jake?" Jimmy asks, pulling himself away from the wrestling match, where men look like they're having a Roman orgy in spandex jockstraps. He gives her a friendly shrug. Suddenly Jimmy the Nice Bartender reminds Donna of Rodney Dangerfield. "Not much. Works hard. Stops here in between double shifts sometimes."

"What's he do?"

"Some upstate outfit. He drives a big old trash truck."

Instead of going *kah-chunk,* Tetris goes haywire. The geometric shapes turn in on themselves, spin around — some even reverse and go up, which is impossible — or is it? Is it possible? But wait a minute. That Neanderthal fantasizes about squishing gay people and bicyclists on the street. How do you suppose he feels about squishing a cop in a Smart Car? He also brags about his preference for women with big butts. Could it be? She can picture Esther Esterhauser sitting in the Fibonacci trailer office on her unnaturally huge derrière with that round face and that soprano voice as she giggles about not wanting to accept an invitation to fly in a biplane.

Donna decides on a different tactic to flush more information from Jimmy the Nice Bartender. There are certain people you should never overload with questions. One straightforward inquiry too many and they clam up. Bartenders are on that list, along with priests, doctors, doormen . . . and former cops.

"Well, Jimmy, all I can say is — I doubt it. I mean I really doubt it." Confused, he leans in to her a little bit, smiling. But she knows he'd rather be left alone to watch the Roman orgy. "I mean, I like him," she says in confidence, "but geesh. I don't know."

"Waz a-matter?"

"He says he's got some old-timey airplane. Offered to take me flying over the Catskills. I don't know about that."

"Oh, yeah. He told me once. He's got a couple of restored old biplanes upstate somewheres." Jimmy shrugs at her. "Hey, if he's got a license — what's the problem? Look at it this way, while he's flying — he's gotta keep both hands on the controls, right?"

"I guess you're right, Jimmy. I guess you're right."

6
THAT'S REALLY STUPID

"Hey partner, am I hearing this correctly?" Conner asks. "The bald man who just went into the liquor store is the loser who was hitting on you *and* he's the same nut-job who tried to turn us both into road kill?"

Before she can turn away from the bartender to whisper a response, Conner continues his narration of the scene.

"Yet another development," he reports. "The liquor store clerk just flipped over the OPEN sign on the door. It now reads CLOSED. They're supposed to be open until 10 P.M. and it's only a little past seven o'clock."

Donna puts a fiver on the bar as a tip, picks up her beer, and switches to a barstool looking out of the open front window, a vantage point that allows her to keep an eye on the street. She can even see the open slat in Conner's maroon venetian blinds. There's the white Rolls parked in front and there's the Italian pasta joint across the street where the fettuccini Alfredo is pretty good and where some low-level Mob guy got zipped decades ago.

"Okay, Fibonacci just walked out to the Rolls," says Conner into her ear. "He's toting a cardboard box. Now he's opening the trunk."

Donna sees Joe Fibonacci putting the box into the car's huge trunk. She can see too that it's not extremely heavy. Once the trunk is loaded, he returns to the liquor store.

Suddenly the air is filled with a jarring beep-beeping noise.

"The sidewalk grate is opening and here comes that elevator-lift," Conner announces.

BRUNKK goes the lift platform as it grinds to a halt at sidewalk level. *BLAMM* goes the metal ramp that drops to the sidewalk.

"Why, if it isn't your good friend Jake rising up from the depths."

Donna watches from the bar window as Conner continues his narration. Jake rides to the sidewalk with a rolling trash Dumpster, which he maneuvers to the curb, then returns to the lift and rides back down to the cellar — only to return moments later with a second rollaway Dumpster, which he also pushes to the edge of the sidewalk. He repeats the action twice more, stopping only when there are four olive-green metal Dumpsters lined up at the curb, oversized wagons, each about the size of a large washing machine.

Donna can tell by the way Jake easily rolls them without putting any muscle into the job that they're empty, which is odd. Why roll an empty Dumpster to the sidewalk? And more importantly — why roll out four of them?

Once all four Dumpsters stand at the sidewalk's edge, a Fibonacci trash truck glides up as if on cue, its powerful air breaks hissing when the wheels lurch to a noisy stop.

Donna cups her mouth with both hands as she pretends to take a sip of her beer: "Hey, partner, I'm in the window of the bar. I can see what's going on. You can stop your narration for now."

"Oh, I see you," Conner says. "Okay, I'll button up."

They both watch as Motty steps down from the truck cab to join Jake on the sidewalk, where the two men confer. Jake does most of the talking while Motty nods a lot. Donna strains to hear what's being said, but there's too much noise from passing traffic.

Once the sidewalk meeting concludes, more interesting stuff begins.

At the rear of the truck, Motty pushes one lever down and jams another up to make the packer blade rise with an irritating grinding noise, revealing the interior storage area — normally a space where tons of putrid garbage and jagged residential refuse are tightly entombed. Once the packer blade is fully risen, Donna can see from her perch in the bar window that the truck's storage chamber is empty, except for a pile of black plastic trash bags — uncrushed.

Jake hoists the two nearest bags by their securely tied necks and drops them into the nearest Dumpster. He tops it with a third bag, which puffs past the edge of the Dumpster like a large black marshmallow in a giant cup of hot chocolate. That's when Motty takes over. He gently taps down the puffy edges of the third bag as he rolls the Dumpster across the sidewalk to the platform in the open grating, then pushes the red DOWN button making the mini-elevator descend into the cellar as it sings out with its beep-beep warning signal. As he is lowered along with the Dumpster, Motty pulls the edges of his white fox fur tightly to his legs so they do not scrape the wall or get hung up in the mechanics of the lift.

While Motty is in the cellar, Jakes fills the second Dumpster, also with three bags.

What kind of trash truck *delivers* the garbage instead of picking it up? *One that carries dope, that's what kind.* Donna cannot believe what's she's witnessing. It's a major narcotics delivery taking place in plain sight, so utterly casual it's brilliant, and she has a ringside seat.

She contemplates doing a mega-cop thing — pulling a one-woman bust by rushing to the sidewalk, her pink .38 caliber Smith & Wesson drawn, aimed with deadly accuracy as she squats into the proper firing stance, just like Starsky or Hutch.

Uh . . . no. Hang on. That may not be such a good idea. They've probably got bigger guns than she does, and they certainly have a perfect place to make her conveniently disappear — a gaping hole in the sidewalk, down which she can be pushed or tossed, only to end up moldering under a pile of corroding pizza boxes at the huge dump in Port Juttistown.

When Motty returns to retrieve the second Dumpster, Jakes fills the third.

One delivers the goods while the other keeps tabs on the street and the remaining goods yet to be delivered. It's clear that they've done this before. Three bags per

Dumpster, four Dumpsters — that equals 12 garbage bags filled with illegal stuff. This will definitely get her back on homicide.

Suddenly Conner breaks the silence.

"Hey partner, I've got an idea, but I may not be able to hear you for a while, so watch my back. Okay?"

Huh?

Within seconds he's on the sidewalk, striding past her like a happy daytime soap actor making an entrance into some ridiculous scene of vampire schmaltz. He glances in at her sitting in the window of O'Toole's, gives her a big wink, and strolls past before she can wave him in, tell him to stand down, back off, don't do this — *What are you, nuts?*

She strains, leaning past the window's edge as Conner ambles past Jake, who stands at the rear of the truck guarding Dumpster number three, which is filled, and the final three bags still in the truck that will ultimately go into Dumpster number four.

The beep-beep of the mini-elevator resumes, a signal that Motty is returning to the surface to retrieve the third rollaway. Before the fluffy white collar of Motty's fur coat can be seen rising above sidewalk level, Conner halts behind Dumpster number four, where, out of Jake's vision, he deftly lifts first one leg, then the other, and steps into the empty container. Once inside, he drops down like a jack-in-the-box clown moving in reverse.

Madre di Dio!

For the second time since the truck arrived, Donna cannot believe what is happening. She had no idea that Conner Anderson is this stupid. What did he go to college for? Now, he probably won't live long enough to benefit from her book. She may have to dedicate it to his memory.

It's all her fault. This is what happens when you let a civilian play cop. She should have known better. Suddenly, instead of an atta-boy and a return to case work, Donna envisions departmental charges and a full bust in rank back to uniformed patrol. She might even end up on traffic duty, directing the flow of commuter buses into the Lincoln Tunnel. And if Conner is killed, narcotic bust or no narcotic bust, she'll be lucky to have that much of a cop job.

Donna feels like she's suffocating. The world is suddenly moving in slow motion.

Motty retrieves Dumpster number three and rides the lift back to the cellar.

Jake pulls the fourth Dumpster from the side of the truck to the rear near the packer blade where, mercifully without so much as a glance inside, he plops his three black garbage bags — one, two, three — onto the curled-up body of TV actor Conner Anderson, who is lying concealed in the bottom. A moment later Motty returns for the final Dumpster which, like the previous three, gets rolled to the lift, then lowered below sidewalk level, followed this time by the slamming of the double doors, which completes the whole operation with a resounding *CLANG*.

Donna's lungs are set to burst.

Conner was up here — now he's suddenly down there. It's as though she's underwater, losing her grip, feeling her life ebb away. This is exactly what she feared most. A crime has been committed in plain sight. Now that crime is concluded — only to spark a far more serious crime that will be concealed beneath the streets of Greenwich Village.

Come on — breathe, think.

After lowering the packer blade in the rear of the truck, Jake strolls across the sidewalk to the liquor store. Taking a chance on being seen, Donna leans out even farther to watch as he opens the door and disappears inside the store that is now closed to the public.

She leans back, returning her butt to the barstool. Finally, with no other option, she consciously wills her brain to send a message to her lungs — *exhale!*

7
Down Under — Rig for Silent Running

Pot!

No question about it — it's marijuana. Even though the trash bags are made of heavy-duty plastic, Conner can smell the overwhelming aroma of freshly cut cannabis. Of course he can smell the contents — after all, he's curled into a fetal position, lying at the bottom of an industrial bucket and buried under three heavy sacks of the stuff. There must be 60 pounds of it spread out on top of him like giant fluffy pillows.

Now I know how the banana feels when three scoops of ice cream are dumped on top, the actor thinks, failing to remember that in the making of a banana split — the banana is always sliced down the middle before being slathered with ice cream and all the other junk: wet nuts, pineapple, whipped cream, and a maraschino cherry.

He delicately adjusts his right leg so the flashlight in his hip pocket stops poking the small of his back. He congratulates himself for having the forethought to grab it before leaving his apartment. It's a long, yellow-rubber flashlight called The Worker's Torch. With four batteries instead of the usual two, it's a powerful light and will come in handy if the Fibonacci thugs leave him alone in the cellar long enough for him to climb out of the Dumpster and poke around, look for blood stains or dead bodies, shoot some video with his cell phone, then — *voilà* — pop out inside O'Toole's Bar as though he'd been there all along and was just returning to the bar after a trip to the bathroom. That's his plan, and won't Donna be impressed when he joins her at the bar with all her investigative work done for her? Then she would owe him a big favor. She'd be back on homicide, and the case of the apartment burglary on August 4th at 221 1/2 Eighth Avenue, apartment 4 will be — better be — *numero uno* on her detective's agenda.

He's moving again. His Dumpster is being pushed in the cellar; he can feel it clanging along a concrete floor, followed by the pull of inertia as it turns a corner, then *WHAM* — it comes to a sudden stop as all four Dumpsters are jammed hard against one another like a train of mini boxcars.

Ouch. That hurt the top of his head.

He can hear voices but cannot make out what's being said. But some muffled words with hard consonants trickle down to him in the Dumpster as they're spoken by men with deep voices moving about in a cellar with a concrete floor and poor acoustics: "Monday delivery," "Billy," "Jimmy," and "DeWayne" are among the words Conner can make out. And there are strings of four-letter words, easy enough to know without hearing every syllable as they trail on in a familiar lilt like a long-memorized nursery rhyme: "Jesus-inaudible . . . piece o'-inaudible . . . inaudible-sucking . . . inaudible-fucking . . . God-inaudible . . . inaudible bitch."

Conner gets the sense that much of the hemorrhaging vitriol is directed at the man named DeWayne. He runs down the cast of characters that he and Donna are familiar with: there's the boss, Joe Fibonacci; Motty, the black man who wears a fur coat in August; and Jake the bald-headed loser, who was hitting on Donna just a few minutes ago inside O'Toole's. Then there's Billy the Mean Bartender and Jimmy the Nice Bartender who owns O'Toole's Bar because Tommy O'Toole died of a heart attack.

Nope. There isn't anyone named De-

Wayne on that list.

Suddenly the weight atop him is lessened and the voices trickle down with more clarity: "That sonova-bitch DeWayne shudda know'd betta . . . inaudible . . . hey Joe, I inaudible that sonova-bitch . . . you ever need . . . inaudible . . . bumped and dumped . . . inaudible-fucker."

A moment later, just as suddenly, the weight atop Conner is lessened again and the voices become even more clear: "That'll teach the bastard . . . the cops don't know shit . . . don't worry . . . inaudible . . . whoever was in that . . . inaudible . . . teeny-ass little car ain't never coming back . . . they probably weren't even cops . . . and even if they were cops . . . inaudible . . . they'll never find that shitbag DeWayne taking a trash nap under ten tons of shit hauled from New York Fucking City."

Uh-oh.

Conner runs down the list of possibilities and comes up with four perfectly obvious facts. First, it is dangerously clear they are removing the bags of pot from the Dumpsters, which is why he's feeling less weight and hearing more of their poetic banter. Second, Jake is definitely the trash truck driver who tried to squish them in front of the Dutch Point Nuclear Power Plant.

251

Third, DeWayne is the poor bastard they saw Friday night, the man standing guard beside the Rolls who got summoned into the liquor store, then got "bumped and dumped." And fourth, Conner may be seconds away from becoming the second bump-and-dump victim of this gang of garbage-hauling dope dealers.

One bag remains atop him. If that one is removed, he'll be exposed — just lying there, helpless, like some bug uncovered at the bottom of the sugar bowl.

The pending danger injects Conner with aberrant thoughts. He pictures his sister and mother in Tupelo, who will cry and wonder what this means for the future of his dad's business. He pictures Uncle Sammy, who will probably just smirk and laugh. He wonders if the cast of *Vampire Love Nest* will hold a moment of silence in his honor. And he can vividly see Donna Prima sitting in the window of O'Toole's Bar — not believing what she's seeing as he strolled past her.

Schwoop.

There goes the final bag, leaving him totally exposed. Conner feels a surge of cool, fresh air. He can tell it's Motty, because it's a pair of white-fur-coated arms that yanks the amorphous thing from atop him in the Dumpster. Fortunately, the bag covers Motty's face as he hoists it awkwardly aloft and turns around. As it rises and disappears, it looks like one of those giant beanbag chairs from the Seventies.

"This is the last one, boss," says Motty.

"No more room in the shed," Jake says. "Maybe we can just put it back in the can, leave it there, cover it up with some garbage. Nobody'll know."

"Brilliant," Fibonacci sneers. "Let's just leave fifty grand worth of product lying under a pile of trash. Maybe that asshole bartender Jimmy will toss it out with the rest of his garbage. You know, Jake, you're scary sometimes. Give it to me. I'll take it upstairs. Billy's waiting in the back room with Freckles Frank. He's gonna start packaging this for small-bag retail. And we got people coming from Brooklyn and Jersey any minute now for wholesale pickup. Keep two bags out, one for each of 'em. Lock up the rest in the shed."

"Right," Motty says obediently.

"You two stay here in case Jimmy wanders down here."

"Okay, boss," says Jake. "Hey boss, don't worry about Jimmy. I mean, I like him okay and all that. He may be a retired cop, but he does have Irish blood. But if I have to —

I'll kill him," Jake continues, trying to prove his worth to Fibonacci as the boss ascends the steps to the liquor store. "If he comes trotting down here while we're conducting our business, we'll just have to hammer the old bastard. Just like you did to DeWayne. With my truck outside — I'll do the hauling o' the dead this time."

"And stay away from them beer lines," Fibonacci calls, halfway up the steps, ignoring Jake's oaths of loyalty. "The last thing we need now is for Jimmy to come down here to inspect his tap lines. Anybody wants a beer — go up there and buy one after we're done."

"Right," says Motty.

"I plan on that! I was moving in on some classy ass when you called," Jake boasts.

"And back me up with these people," Fibonacci shouts down the trap door behind the liquor store sales counter. "Especially Jersey. They're from Atlantic City. I don't know 'em too good. And Motty, hurry up with that other piece of business because they'll be here any minute."

"Right, boss." Motty has just enough time to acknowledge Fibonacci's final comment before the trap door slams shut.

Uncovered in the bottom of Dumpster number four, essentially naked to the men

he now knows to be murdering drug dealers, Conner can hear every word with
crystal clarity. The only voice he has recognized is Jake's, but it's obvious the other
two voices belong to Motty and Fibonacci.
He hears the crinkling sound of the giant
beanbags being hoisted, scraped across the
floor, and placed somewhere in the direction of the steps leading up to the liquor
store. A door squeaks and latches closed.
The metallic sound of a padlock snaps shut.

"Hey Jake, did ya hear about what happened after I popped DeWayne Friday
night?" Motty's deep voice echoes through
the cellar in distinct African-American dia-
lect.

"What?"

"Trouble. Cop trouble. Lots of it. The
boss got pretty bent about it."

"He didn't say nothing to me, Motty."

"Yeah. DeWayne was not cool about gettin' whacked. He did not care for the experience, believe me. After the first shot, he
started screamin' and fightin' and shit. I
couldn't believe it, man. I had to pop him
half a dozen times just to get him to calm
down so he could die."

"Damn."

"Some people living over the store made
the call. A crap-load of cops showed up,

nosing all around. Joe had to move the Rolls in a hurry and I had to wait down here with DeWayne lying right there where he dropped. Even then he was still groanin' and bleedin' and shit. And me, just standing here trying not to breathe too loud and hoping he'd die 'cause I sure as hell couldn't do no more shootin'."

"Damn."

"Yeah. I was scared of gettin' nabbed, man. No lie."

"Good thing the trap door was shut."

"Yeah. And Freckles Frank did good. He talked some good shit. He convinced the cops it was only loud gangsta rap on his iPod that he had plugged into the store's Bose Wave."

"Smart thinking! Freckles Frank is smart," Jake says. "He's going to NYU, ya know. Studying business."

"Yeah, I know. But Joe was really ticked about the whole thing. So he bought me a new toy."

"What's that?"

"This." Motty withdraws a long-barreled .357 from deep inside the pocket of his full-length white fox fur coat.

"A silencer! Nice. It looks good on the end of that Winchester. That must have cost a pretty penny. Does Joe want us to go upstairs and take care of those people who called the cops? Make sure they never bother us again?"

"Not exactly."

"What then?"

"He wants me to take care of *you*." There is a long silence. "You shudda never done it, Jake. We found some o' the missing shit in your truck. It wasn't just DeWayne double-crossing the team. You was in it with him. Freelancing ain't allowed, you know that."

Another long silence follows.

"And on top o' that, you ought not go 'round trying to crush teeny-tiny cars, even if they was cops. Man, that was really some stupid shit. You act odd sometimes, you know that, Jake? Besides, donchu know there's cameras all over that fuckin' power plant? Even the squirrels in the trees got little cameras strapped to their heads." Another silence. "Anyway, Joe don't want to take no chances."

"Listen . . . Motty . . ."

"Never mind all that, Jake. I gotta do this before Jersey and Brooklyn show up for their pickup. Then I gotta go home, man. I'm tired and I gotta long drive ahead of me. You know how long it takes to get across the G.W. and up the Thruway at this hour."

"Listen, Motty . . ."

Burh-rift!

The burping gunshot makes a waffling noise, like high-pressure air shooting through a tube with only the hint of an ordinary "pop" normally made by a handgun's discharge. The sound is followed by a distinct thump. That's Jake hitting the concrete floor, Conner thinks. There is a moment of silence. Just as a low hissing groan bubbles from Jake's throat, there come two more waffling burps — a pair of *coup de grace* shots, Conner figures.

The groaning stops.

8
STILL DOWN UNDER

"Jersey! Bag one!"

The voice of Joe Fibonacci calls down from the liquor store just moments after Motty finishes dumping Jake's body into one of the four Dumpsters. Thankfully he did not select the one holding the curled-up Conner Anderson.

"Right, boss."

Moments later the voice comes again.

"Brooklyn! Bag two."

"Right, boss."

After their upstairs business is concluded, both Fibonacci and Motty return to the basement.

"Good job," says Fibonacci, peering into the metal coffin where Jake's cadaver lies, his left foot unnaturally wrapped around the top of his head. "He won't be double-crossing us anymore."

"And he won't be trying to run down any more cops, or sanitation inspectors, or whatever those two were in that joke of a car."

"You believe that shit?" Fibonacci asks Motty. "He hears that some cops are nosing around, so he takes it on himself to follow them, wait for 'em to finish breakfast at the Port J Diner, then tries to run over 'em right in front of the nuke plant."

"And botches the job."

"Yeah, well, thank God he botched it. All we need is a bunch of cops and paranoid Feds worried about nuclear shit poking around our business. What a loser."

They push the Dumpster bearing the dead Jake to the elevator and slide it onto the elevator ramp.

"You take him up to the sidewalk and load him into his truck, pack him down, then drive it to the Con Ed lot on Seventh Avenue and park it," Fibonacci instructs. "I'll pick you up there in the Rolls in a couple of minutes. Tomorrow I'll report both him and the truck missing. Let the city cops find him. They'll think it's some Mob hit."

They are the final words Conner hears. Fibonacci ascends the steps to the liquor store and slams the trap door. Motty switches off the single naked overhead light-bulb in the ceiling, rides the lift up with the

Dumpster, dumps the body, pushes the Dumpster back to the sidewalk lift, and pushes the DOWN button. The Dumpster returns to the cellar by itself followed by the noise of the sidewalk ramp as it clangs shut.

Conner is left alone in the dark.

Anxious to get out and stretch his cramped legs, he waits an obligatory moment to make certain no one is around, then tugs The Worker's Torch from his hip pocket, rolls onto all fours, and cautiously raises his eyes past the metal rim of the Dumpster to peer into the blackness. He clicks on the flashlight and waves it across the room.

To the left is the empty Dumpster sitting stationary on the lift platform.

In the middle of the room, the floor is wet with blood turning dark brown as it mixes with little rivulets of beer oozing from the caps of a dozen metal barrels, from which a spaghetti-jumble of clear tubing rises through the ceiling to connect with the tap handles in O'Toole's Bar. It's not much of a blood puddle, at least not much for a man shot three times, and it certainly does not qualify as the classic "pool of blood." There's no gore, no guts — just a little reddish-brown stain mixed with stale beer, all of it seeping toward the drainage grate in the middle of the smelly, sticky floor.

On the other side of the stain is the shed. It's not a real tool-shed, not like the ones sold at Home Depot. It's a makeshift thing the size of a small closet, framed by 2 × 4's and covered with chicken wire. Conner holds the flashlight steady. Inside, past the padlocked door, he counts the outline of nine black beanbag sacks. That would be the correct number, he thinks. Four Dumpsters, each with three bags; one bag taken upstairs for retail, the other two sold wholesale — one to Jersey and one to Brooklyn.

His knees aching, Conner twists in his metal crib to wave the flashlight at the dark space behind him, where scores of beer cases are stacked high like columns of Tinker Toys, some laden with full bottles of beer, some empty. The whole cellar reeks of the sour odor of hops and malt and fetid alcohol.

He twists tighter in the compact space to focus The Worker's Torch into the far corner behind him.

There it is.

He climbs from the Dumpster with far less alacrity than he entered it and limps with cramped legs to the *other* narrow staircase in the far back corner, ascends to the trap door, which he pushes up, and then steps into the small, dark inner office of O'Toole's Bar.

Phew, nobody's home.

Conner quietly closes the trap behind him, then unlatches and slowly pulls open the heavy metal door to the small hallway. His ears are instantly assaulted with The Dave Clark Five's version of "Do You Love Me?"

No one's in the corridor. Good.

He steps past the metal door, walks through the corridor and into the bar where Jimmy the Nice Bartender is intently focused on a televised wrestling match. Assuming he's returning from the toilet, the others take no notice of him.

From the gut, Mike Smith is belting "Well . . . do you lov-v-v-e me?" while Dave Clark plays the drums like a wild man in a *Tarzan* movie.

And there she is.

New York City Police Detective Donna Prima is still sitting in the window, but Conner knows from her body language that she is a coiled spring. She is straining at the open window, watching events surrounding the trash truck still parked at the curb, and there — in her right hand — is her pink .38. She's concealing it with her left forearm, but it's still visible. So far, no one else has noticed.

The engine of the trash truck cranks to life, sending smoke pouring from the vertical muffler rising just behind the driver's cab. Donna stands, ready to bolt from the bar, gun in hand, and rush the truck to prevent it from driving away. Seeing that she is ready to leap into action, Conner hurries up behind her to stop her exit.

"Hello, Detective Prima. So nice to see you again." He gently pushes the wrist of her gun hand down, deftly concealing the pink metal from sight.

Donna is so startled she cannot even curse — not even in Italian. The words just don't come. Suddenly the trash truck backfires like a firecracker, drawing their attention to it. They watch as it pulls away from the curb, its muffler belching black smoke. Donna turns back to Conner, her eyes bulging with a multitude of emotions, the two principal ones being anger and relief. She is still unable to speak.

"Let's sit and have a beer," he says as calmly as he can. "I have so much to tell you."

Donna slides back onto the barstool and returns her pistol to the ankle holster. Conner helps himself to a deep, long swig of amber liquid from Donna's lukewarm Bud-weiser. Finally, Donna finds her voice.

"I thought that was you getting poured out of that Dumpster into the trash truck," she says.

"You saw a body?"

"Part of one."

"What part?"

"Legs. And they bent the wrong way when Motty jammed down the packer blade. I thought it was you." She looks down at his legs.

"Not me. Both of my legs are right where they're supposed to be."

"Well, whose body was it?"

"I don't know his last name, but I believe he goes by the first name of Jake. That's who you saw getting dumped. Motty shot him with his new toy — a silencer."

Donna stares in disbelief. Her eyes fill with water. The D.C. Five's lead singer, Mike Smith, is still belting from the gut: "Well . . . do you love me?"

9
ON THE ROAD AGAIN

"I just hope you're right," Conner says, shouting to be heard over the roar of the engine as they bounce west on the Interstate, in the trash truck with a biplane hood ornament.

"Why wouldn't I be right? I told you before, we need to get inside that dump. What better way is there? With this thing, we simply drive right through the front gate. It's brilliant. I'm glad I thought of it," Donna says, only half joking.

"Yeah, but the Trojan horse wasn't toting a dead guy like we are. There's probably a law against it. Maybe you should call it in."

"I'll call it in later. After we get more goods on this gang. And what was that about a horse?" Conner looks at her from the passenger seat. This is no time for a lesson on ancient literature.

"Never mind. Listen, I'm serious, what if they stop us?"

"Who's going to stop us?"

"Well, if the cops don't stop us, then how about Motty the Fur Man who has a big gun with a silencer, or Joe Fibonacci who tells Motty the Fur Man to kill people with his big gun with a silencer? If either of them sees this truck tooling around in their backyard — won't they assume something's up after they parked it in a Con Ed lot a block away from O'Toole's Bar, with Jake's dead body in the trash bay?"

Donna shrugs. "Maybe they'll think the truck is haunted — that Jake has turned into a vampire-zombie and he's coming after 'em. You can handle that. That's your line of work, isn't it?"

"Great. The *really* scary thing is — that may actually be the best we can hope for."

"Don't worry about it," Donna says with a sly half smile, firmly gripping the large steering wheel on a curve in the road. "Besides, they're ready for beddie-bye. I keep telling you, even thugs and dopers want to go home and watch *Seinfeld* reruns at the end of a long day. And don't forget, I'm still a cop. We'll turn the dead guy over to homicide after I get the scoop on these jokers." She brakes and downshifts for slow traffic and maneuvers to pass an 18-wheeler bearing the familiar Walmart logo.

"How'd you learn to drive a thing like this anyway?" Conner asks.

"My dad. He loves trucks."

"Don't tell me your firefighter father taught you how to drive the ladder truck."

"Nope. That would invite serious trouble. But I did sit behind the wheel bunches of times. He taught me the gears. Did I ever tell you about my dad's favorite kind of fire?"

"I don't believe you did."

"Liquor store."

"Liquor store? How come?"

"Because the boots that firefighters wear are big at the top. Big enough to conceal two bottles per leg. A call to a liquor store was everybody's favorite. They all went home happy."

They bounce along in silence, occasionally exchanging glances — each knowing that the other is thinking about something other than progress on the case. They're thinking about romance — about sex certainly, but also about something bigger than sex, which makes them each a little flustered, a little flush with curiosity, and a touch circumspect.

After an hour on the road, the foothills of the verdant Catskill Mountains come slowly into view. This is the area where the Woodstock rock festival was held. It's the land where the Jewish resorts were once located, where all those chubby, old-time comedians got their start before television. It's also where mobsters from New York City used to go to get away from it all, when they needed a break from the daily grind of knee-capping, extortion, and murder. Of course, they sometimes toted dead bodies up here in the trunks of their cars — bodies that usually got dumped in the woods, left as food for the bears. There are lots of bears in the Catskills. They generally don't eat meat, but they are omnivores after all, and are happy to eat the meat of jettisoned dead mobsters when it's on the menu.

Staring at the road ahead of her, Donna breaks the silence.

"I've got to tell you something, Vampire Man."

"What's that?"

"My claustro was really kicking in."

"Your what?"

"Claustrophobia. I'm claustro in a bad way. That's why your little golf cart of a car freaked me so bad."

"Seriously?"

"Yeah. And it happened again while you were in that Dumpster. You know, that oversized metal tissue box on wheels, which

I have already told you was the stupidest thing I have ever seen any human being do. And I have seen people do some pretty stupid stuff. It is, after all, the subject of my book." She turns to glare hard at him. "Anyway, while I was sitting there wondering if I should call in the cavalry or just charge in myself — I was sweating with the claustro. No lie. I was having a *real* attack. A major one. That's never happened to me before. It wasn't *me* buried in a Dumpster — *you* were. But I was picturing you lying in such a tiny space and it gave me one of the worst attacks I've ever had. I mean, I was *really* paralyzed. Just the idea of it, the idea of you suffering, it hammered me. I couldn't breathe. I had to force my lungs to exhale. I must have lost two pounds just sitting there sweating it out. I confess, it may be the reason why I *didn't* jump in and do something to save you."

She looks at the road stretching in front of the truck as she speaks. Conner knows she's trying to tell him that she actually cares about what happens to him, which is as big a stunner for her as it is for him. He senses not to push it, to just let the thing unravel at its own pace. If some kind of psychokinetic, telepathic claustrophobia can be an expression of love — so be it. After a long pause, Conner breaks the silence.

"Okay, now it's my turn. There's one part of the whole thing that I failed to tell you."

"Yeah?"

"Well," he takes a long breath, "while I was stuck in there, I realized how big an idiot I had been and I regretted it. Impending death has a way of telling you what's important and what isn't. One of my thoughts, in addition to not wanting to die, was how pissed you'd be at me for getting killed. It's weird, but that's all I could think of. And I decided that if I had to get bumped by those jokers, I wanted to sail out of this world while thinking of you."

Without looking directly at her, Conner can see Donna give a small nod of acknowledgment. It may have been no more than a twitch of her taut facial muscles, such a compact movement that she may not have been aware of making it. But it was there. Conner saw it. And it tells him that she appreciates his intimate confession just as much as he appreciated hers.

They speak little during the balance of the drive to Port Juttistown. The trash truck is noisy, but they are untroubled by it. Eventually, they turn onto smaller county roads toward the west, where the sun is in the final stages of setting and the stark orange glare requires them to pull down the blinder shields that hang over the window. They are immersed now in the rolling hills of the Catskills, which spread out in all directions. Here and there, majestic houses sit alone in grandeur atop a hill; elsewhere there are clusters of exhausted-looking homes and trailers — what salesman call "mobile homes." And there are rights-of-way cut through the trees that crest the hills in the distance, unnatural cleavages in the natural growth where mean-looking pylons rise every 200 yards, bearing cables that deliver electricity south to New York City.

"Hey, why don't you check the glove compartment?" Donna suggests casually.

Conner clicks on the cab's interior light and pulls the compartment's handle. As he does so, an automatic handgun tumbles from the overstuffed compartment. The actor catches it before it hits the floor.

"I thought so," Donna says.

"I bet Jake regrets not having this with him in the cellar this evening. Not that he's capable of regret." He hands the large automatic weapon to Donna and continues to rifle the compartment, which is stuffed with papers, maps, a multitool, a large uneaten submarine sandwich turning moldy in a plastic baggie, and a pamphlet titled

"Retirement in County Clare, Ireland."

Donna notes the manufacturer of the gun as she examines it with one hand while keeping the steering wheel steady with the other. "SIG Sauer. These boys like nice toys." She wonders if ballistics testing on it will solve any unsolved murders.

Behind the sandwich wrapper is another much larger plastic bag, which Conner tugs loose — sending a confetti of gasoline charge-receipts tumbling to the floor.

"And here we have Exhibit A," he pronounces, holding it up in the light. "Pot . . . weed . . . grass . . . ganja . . . Mary Jane." He jiggles the bag in the air. "This is why they whacked him. Jake and DeWayne were stealing. There must be half a pound in here."

"That's a Class D felony," Donna says. "One to seven in the state pen."

Conner opens the bag and inhales. "Very fresh. Should I put it back?"

"Yeah. And put the SIG back too."

"What do you think was in that box that Fibonacci loaded into the trunk of the Rolls?"

"Money," Donna tells him. "Cash. The pot went in. The money came out."

"Of course — duh."

"You said Billy Average the Mean Bartender was there?"

"I heard Fibonacci say he was. He said Billy and somebody they called Freckles Frank were upstairs in the back room of the liquor store, packaging for small-bag retail. That's what he said."

"Yeah. Billy must've had the week's receipts all boxed up and waiting in the liquor store. They could only work through the liquor store tonight because Jimmy was tending bar, so they couldn't take any chances. That meant temporarily shutting the liquor store. It's inconvenient, but they had to do it because Jimmy the Nice Bartender is not a part of the gang. That's good. I mean, he *is* a retired cop, even if he's too stupid to know what's going on right under his own nose."

Once again they ride in silence, turning from the county highway to smaller, slower roads that wind their way to the outskirts of Port Juttistown. Finally they come to the unmarked drive that turns into the wooded lane leading to the gate of the Fibonacci compound and the immense trash dump stretching behind it. They make the turn and climb the narrow path into the woods. At the clearing about halfway to the gate, a herd of white-tailed deer look up with idle interest, their brightly flagged tails flopping contentedly. Familiar with the sight of trash trucks, none of them bolt for the cover of the forest, but instead dip back to the ground to resume foraging.

At the hilltop, the truck stops at the chain-link fence where a low-hanging fog is rolling in, obscuring visibility. Donna clicks on the high beams. The gate is bound with a heavy chain cinching tight the two metal gates and secured shut with a silver padlock the size of a man's fist. She turns off the engine and the two stare blankly at the locked gates.

"You may be right," Conner says in the darkness of the truck's cab as they strain to see if anyone is around.

"Right about what?"

"About zombies. That fog is creepy. This could be the place where the dead really do reanimate."

"In that case, we're the perfect team."

"How's that?"

"I'm a cop. You're a vampire. Who better to investigate 'The Dump of the Living Dead?' "

"Very funny."

"Shh, you hear that?" Donna asks, putting her hand on Conner's forearm. They listen quietly for a moment.

"I don't hear a thing," he says.

"Shh. There it is again. You don't hear something tapping?"

"No. What tapping?"

Tap-tap-tap. The sound is very slight, almost inaudible.

"That!" She grips the handle of The Worker's Torch, her thumb on the rubber button, making ready to turn it on fast. He rolls the passenger window halfway down and listens intently to the darkness.

"I don't hear anything out there except crickets and frogs."

Tap-tap-tap.

"You don't hear that?"

"Uh . . ."

"Well *I* hear it," she says. "And it sounds like it's coming from the back of the truck. Are you sure Jake is really dead?"

Unable to see her in the dark, he looks in her direction. "Well, he took three bullets, moaned, stopped moaning, started a death rattle, stopped the death rattle, got poured in a Dumpster, and got stuffed into a garbage truck where, according to you, his legs were bent the wrong way."

"Well, if he's really dead — then who's making that tapping noise in the back of the truck?"

The noise comes yet again, this time much louder: *Tap-tap-tap.*

"Uh-h-h . . ." Conner begins, feeling uncomfortable. "Yeah, I hear it. Uh . . . I uh. . . ."

That's when Donna plays her hand. She clicks on The Worker's Torch directly under her chin as she leans her ghostly illuminated face into the soap opera actor and shrieks like a devilish barn owl intent upon drawing blood from its prey. Conner instantly recoils against the door and howls in fear. He instinctively unlatches the passenger door and exits the truck the fastest way possible — rear-end first. By the time he can stand and brush dirt from his trousers, Donna has clicked on the interior light. She is tossing her head back in a great fit of laughter as her stomach heaves in and out and her fists pound the steering wheel with delight.

"That is *not* funny," Conner protests angrily. She stops laughing just long enough to look at him standing outside, leaning against the open door as he tugs unhappily at a wedgie. "I almost crapped myself!" he shouts. The sight of him sends her into a second round of hooting, howling mirth — this time stomping both feet.

"I can't believe you fell for that," she says between bursts of laughter, pointing an unsympathetic finger at him. With the other hand, she holds the truck's ignition key to display what was actually making the tapping noise. "That's the Mississippi in you. And you know what? That's what you get for scaring me out of my faith in the Virgin birth by climbing into that tin can and making me have a claustro attack."

Conner composes himself. He notices that she's ready and waiting for him to make a comeback so she can retaliate even more triumphantly. She even has one eyebrow arched, an expression he's never seen her make. He decides to stand down. This is her moment — her revenge for his taking matters into his own hands.

"Well, now that you've had your fun, what are you going to do about that locked gate?" he asks, trying to regain his self-respect. "Are we going to smash our way inside?"

Donna's arched eyebrow falls back into place. "Well, let's see," she says, refocusing on the task at hand. She holds up a key chain from which several keys dangle from a figurine of a woman with an extraordinarily bulbous behind.

She selects one key in particular. "Let's try this one." She climbs down from the driver's seat and walks into the high beams, standing aside at the gate so she doesn't block the shaft of light. She inserts the key into the large padlock and turns it clockwise. The lock snaps and flops open. She turns to Conner, who remains in the truck, watching.

"As they say in Denmark — *'voilà.'*"

Conner decides it's best to keep his mouth shut.

10

THE DUMP

OF THE LIVING DEAD

Donna keeps the transmission in low as she slowly steers through the maze. The big wheels lurch around mountains of garbage along dirt pathways made semi-firm by crushed tin cans and tons of crumbled Styrofoam. Up close, some of the mountains look like latter-day pyramids; others are truncated mounds that rise only a dozen feet from a vast base. There are valleys too, wide trenches where the earth has been dug out to make room for trash that has not yet been hauled in to fill the openings.

Within the maze, they rumble past dump trucks, backhoes, and bulldozers parked in out-of-the-way niches — waiting, as though sleeping, for the next day's hard labor to begin. There's a flatbed trailer that holds several industrial-sized generators. One generator runs loudly, cranking out energy via a cable to one lone telephone pole capped by a single floodlight. The eerie beam, cast downward into the fog, illuminates a John Deere Gator, a small vehicle that is essentially a golf cart but shaped like a miniature pickup truck.

The fog continues to roll in, severely limiting their visibility. The high beams become useless because the light simply disappears into an opaque wall of haze, so Donna puts the headlights on low beam to focus on the few feet of ground immediately in front of the truck.

"See any zombies yet?" Donna asks after a half hour of meandering in and out of trash piles.

"No. But that doesn't mean there aren't any. This place gives me the creeps. And don't play any more tricks on me."

"Hey, did you see that?"

"I said no more tricks."

"I'm not playing a trick. I thought I saw something move." Reaching a dead end, she steers the truck as far to one side as she can, even gunning the truck several feet up onto the trash pile so that she can back up and turn around in one smooth effort. The gears make a harsh grinding noise as she struggles to find reverse. "There it is again."

"I didn't see anything. What'd it look like?"

"I'm not sure. I can't see a thing in this

fog. It just looked like something moving, something darting around down there in the mist."

"A bear?"

"No. Smaller than a bear."

"Rats?"

"No. Bigger than a rat."

"Deer?"

"Smaller than a deer. A dog maybe."

"Junkyards have dogs, not garbage dumps," Conner says. "This is a garbage dump." He stares cautiously out of the passenger window, but sees little more than garbage surrounded by clouds of grey haze. "This better not be another joke," he warns.

"I swear upon the grave of Saint Michael the Archangel, patron saint to all police officers, that I am *not* fooling around. I saw movement out there," Donna vows, cramming the shift into first gear and lurching the truck forward again.

Conner impulsively yanks open the glove compartment and withdraws the SIG Sauer.

"Hey! Put that thing back. All you'll do is shoot yourself, or even worse — you'll shoot me." Conner obediently shoves the weapon back into the overstuffed compartment.

Donna shifts into first gear, making the trash truck resume its slow forward momentum. The narrow paths snaking around the mountains of garbage only seem to lead deeper into the mysterious dump. They are still lost, and in this thick fog it's possible they could be wandering all night long. She checks the gas gauge — less than an eighth of a tank. That's not good. And the problem is compounded by the fact that she doesn't really know what she's looking for. If it were a perfectly clear day — she wouldn't know any better. Obviously they're either importing pot or growing it themselves. Using private trash trucks as a means of distribution is brilliant. A trash truck stops everywhere in the City, it goes into alleys, garages, double-parks with impunity, stops traffic while the workers go into cellars. Nobody questions it. But this dump — this is a mystery.

"Hey, I just thought of something," Conner says. "Why do they need generators?"

"I don't follow you?"

"A while back. There was that flatbed trailer. Remember? We squeezed past it near that trash mountain with the light pole next to it. The truck had some great big generators. And one of them was running. What for?"

"Electricity. For the light at the top of that pole."

"That's another thing. Why do they need

a light pole in a dump? Do they work at night? And why do they need several industrial-sized generators to operate a single scoop light?"

"Hmm. Vampire Man, you could be onto something there. You're starting to think like a real detective. The problem is finding it again in this fog."

"I've got an idea," Conner says, brimming with renewed enthusiasm. "This fog is a ground hugger. If I get on the top of the truck, I might be able to see the light on that pole. If so, I can call out directions to you."

"Let's give it a try," she agrees, as her respect for this Southern WASP increases another half notch.

Conner first looks around carefully to make certain there's no mysterious movement outside the passenger door. Once satisfied, he takes a deep breath and opens the door, leans away, and quickly closes it. He shimmies up the side of the truck using the running board and door handle as stepping points. The idea pays off instantly. The fog is only slightly thinner above the truck, but he can indeed see the glow of the floodlight in the distance.

"Forward and generally to the right," he commands. "That's it, now make the first possible left."

He keeps alert for any unusual ground movement while she chugs ahead in first gear. He calls directions like a windjammer sailor shouting directions from the crow's nest. For several minutes Donna obeys, taking it slow on turns and gingerly easing the tires over bumps and into ruts so as not to dislodge her untethered passenger from the roof.

"Now straight on as much as you can go. There it is, just to the right."

From here, no more directions are needed. Donna can see the light atop the pole and she makes a beeline for it, pulling to a halt in front of the flatbed trailer laden with a pair of industrial generators. She shuts off the truck's engine but leaves the headlights shining onto the wall of fog.

Conner climbs down from the top of the truck and Donna joins him as they examine the generators under the glare of the pole light.

"Vampire Man, *you* are a genius! Look at those power cables. What do you see?"

"I see that the generator lines drape over the pole and go down into that pile."

"Yeah. And why does a big-ass pile of garbage need power lines running into it?"

"Electrocuting rats?"

"I doubt it."

"Maybe it's a way of hurrying the decay of biodegradable stuff?" he says. "You know, some chemistry thing."

"I doubt that too. Look, it's mostly plastic garbage bags and metal. And there's the rear end of an old Buick up there. I've never heard of a biodegradable Buick." Donna unconsciously uses her tough cop voice. "Okay," she says, "Turn on that flashlight, let's walk around this pile of shit!"

Taking her elbow, Conner waves the beam of The Worker's Torch in front of them as they circle the trash pyramid in the fog. Donna walks slowly, pausing every few steps while Conner waves the light beam up and down the mountainous slope of garbage bags and jagged, protruding metal. They recognize some of the refuse. Mattresses are easy. So are car fenders and semi-crushed washing machines. There's a bathroom vanity, an old A&P grocery cart, and what appears to be a jet ski poking from the wall of garbage very near the top of the pile and looking like Goldfinger's secret escape rocket ready to blast off.

They're nearly back where they started when she stops, almost directly under the light pole.

"Hello-o-o," she sings out. "What does

that look like to you?" Conner releases his grip on her elbow and clicks off The Worker's Torch in the glow of the powerful overhead scoop.

"It's a giant pipe, like an open sewer culvert."

"Exactly." The motorized Gator cart is parked ten feet beyond the pipe opening. "Tell me something, Vampire Man. Do you think that golf-cart gizmo will fit inside that pipe?"

"Sure. It looks small enough. But why would they want to drive a miniature truck into the middle of a huge pile of trash?"

"Let's find out." Before Conner can think about it, Donna's in the driver's seat of the Gator, cranking its small electric engine with the key in the ignition and spinning it around. "Hop in," she orders. After Conner does so, she turns and drives the little vehicle straight into the dark tunnel leading into the heart of the largest pile of trash in the entire dump of the living dead.

11
INTO THE PILE

The tunnel goes straight for about 20 feet and curves to the right before coming to a dark dead end. The dim headlights of the Gator illuminate a wall of corrugated metal.

"What's that?" Donna asks.

"Looks like a garage door to me."

"Me too. Go open it," she orders.

Conner squeezes sideways past the narrow space between the Gator and the arching tunnel walls, which he realizes are made of durable, reinforced plastic. It really is a prefab sewer culvert. There's no doorknob or handle anywhere on the barrier. He bangs on it with his fist, creating a hollow echo on the other side. The feel lets him know it's made of thin metal. He turns around.

"Maybe there's a remote button somewhere."

"Good thinking. Hang on." She clicks on The Worker's Torch to inspect the recessed compartments in the Gator's dash. "Hey, this thing even has a cup holder," she says. "And instead of a cup in the cup holder, there's this little gizmo. Stand aside."

Donna aims the remote and clicks. The door responds by rising with a deafening clatter of metal rolling past metal and grinds to a halt revealing a wide, brightly illuminated chamber. Conner squints into the blinding glare. He shields his eyes and walks into the cavernous space, oblivious to the steady, low-level noise of the Gator humming directly behind him.

A few short steps into the cavern they both see it all — row after row of marijuana plants growing in long, carefully maintained dirt-filled troughs, all of them illuminated by overhead strips of powerful grow lights that mimic sunshine and project a deep yellowish haze under wide fluorescent reflectors.

Conner selects one long aisle and walks to the middle, studying the greenery as he goes. The plants are clumped by stages of growth. Some troughs are filled with mere seedlings, delicate stems enveloped in nurturing brown mulch. Others hold rows of youthful plants uniformly one foot high, straining with vigor toward the light that hangs above. Still other troughs contain rows of mature plants more than six feet tall — giant flowering clusters of cannabis, each sporting dozens of wide starburst leaves that brim with serrated edges.

"*Santa Madre,*" Donna whispers to herself from the driver's seat of the Gator. She scans the interior, sloping walls, and curved ceiling. "This is some sort of building they've buried under a mountain of trash."

"Yeah," Conner responds, looking up at the corrugated metal ceiling and down the side of the concave wall. "It's an old military Quonset hut, like the garage bay next to the trailer office."

"What's a Quonset hut?"

"Didn't you ever watch *Gomer Pyle?*"

"Of course. Good old classic sitcom. Spin-off of *Andy Griffith,*" she says, not mentioning that Conner sometimes reminds her of Barney Fife even if he does look like a young Sean Connery.

"Right," he says. "Gomer's barracks was a Quonset hut."

"Very smart. Who'd think of looking under a pile of garbage for a hothouse pot factory?"

"Nobody but you and me."

"You got that right, Vampire Man."

Conner walks the full length of the main aisle, stepping over garden hoses stretched along the floor as Donna follows with the Gator. At the end of the building, an open space contains several waist-high counter-tops, a large industrial oven, and an assortment of microwave ovens.

"This must be their post-harvest work-space," Conner says. "I didn't know pot was supposed to be cooked."

"It's not," Donna says. "The best pot is dried in the sun. They're speeding up the process. These guys are in a hurry."

They turn the corner, slowly moving back toward the entrance along the far aisle filled on both sides by arching clusters of mature plants, whose springy leaves seem to bounce with happiness under artificial radiance. Following behind Conner in the Gator, Donna is about to tell him that she's re-minded of her one visit to the Brooklyn Bo-tanic Garden in the eighth grade when a glint of movement catches her eye. Looking behind her, she sees exactly what she sus-pected earlier when she spotted mysterious, ghostly movement in the fog.

They are dogs — two of them.

But they're not just dogs — they're Do-bermans, silent creatures following them in a manner so easygoing they seem like a pair of wiseguys relishing their victims' helpless-ness before launching into an attack of bloody fury.

Donna takes her foot off the little round pedal. The Gator instantly stops. The Dobermans also stop.

"Hey, Vampire Man," she says quietly.

"Look at the size of these monster plants over here," Conner shouts. "They should be displayed at the county fair. These guys would win a wall of blue ribbons!"

"Hey, Vampire Man," Donna says again, in a tone just a little more insistent as the dogs hold a fixed stare upon her. Conner walks on, oblivious to her cues.

"Hydroponics too. Look at this. A whole table with no dirt. They're growing seeds and seedlings in nothing but water."

"Umm, you kinda need to listen to me," Donna says with as much volume as she dares. "I know I promised you, but this is no joke. I found your ghosts. In fact, I think they've been following us since we rolled up the garage door."

When Conner turns, he sees Donna's body oddly cork-screwed in the driver's seat as she looks to the rear. A few feet behind the Gator he sees the two Dobermans sitting on their haunches, waiting with patient confidence for their soon-to-be victims to make their next — and likely last — move. Like Donna, Conner freezes.

"What do we do now?" he asks after a pause.

"Not sure."

"Can you shoot 'em?"

"Do you think they'll *let* me shoot 'em?"

"No, not really," he concedes. "But at least they're not growling."

"I did notice that," Donna says slowly, nodding at the two muscular dogs. "It's almost like they're amused. You know — toying with us."

Conner remembers the way Motty spoke to Jake just before killing him — complaining about feeling tired and having to face heavy traffic during his commute home across the Hudson. "You mean — messing with our heads to make us sweat?" he asks.

"Yeah. Like that."

"They're looking at me like I remind 'em of London broil."

A lightbulb goes off in Donna's head. "That reminds me. You remember that moldy sandwich in the glove compartment of the truck?"

"Yeah?"

"Well, I figured your ghosts would turn out to be dogs, so I tossed the baggie in the back of the Gator. But I figured they'd be noisy beasts, not a pair of silent killers."

"Smart! It's that kind of advance planning

that made you a detective, I'm sure. Can you reach it without irritating our audience?"

"There's only one way to find out," she says, slowly reaching to the back, a gesture that earns cautious attention from the dogs, making them rise to a standing position. Keeping an eye to the rear, Donna unfolds the plastic baggie and withdraws the gamy sandwich, which she can tell is, or used to be, roast beef with Swiss cheese, lettuce, and tomato — except that the Swiss is oozing with wet mold, the tomato has shriveled to near nonexistence, and the lettuce is limp and brown like last week's cut grass. As for the one-inch thickness of meat, well — it still looks at least a little like roast beef. It's all folded into a submarine-shaped chunk of Italian bread that has hardened to the consistency of a slightly rubbery football.

The dogs get the scent of the decaying beef and remove their eyes from Donna and Conner for the first time to look at the thing in her hands — the source of the odor. She considers tossing it. After all, it looks and feels like a football. Why not heave a forward pass as far as she can manage? Let the dogs chase after it while they scoot in the opposite direction. If she could make it land in one of the troughs, or better yet in the branches of one of the big marijuana plants, she could buy them even more time. But she dismisses the idea. The image of the dogs bounding after them and catching them in the darkened sewer culvert is not an outcome either she or her claustrophobia wishes to experience.

Using both hands, she grips the sandwich like a stick of firewood and breaks it in half, tearing at the sinew of the meat as she pulls the whole rotten thing into two parts.

"All righty then," Donna whispers, swinging both arms over the side of the Gator. The dogs watch every action with keen attention.

This is it, she thinks. *Let's hope for the best.*

She decides to speak in a happy voice, the type of deceitfully friendly voice all people use when trying to trick a dog into stopping one behavior or into starting another. But not too loud. She doesn't want to startle them.

"Come and get it, fellas," she says, snapping her wrists to emphasize that the sandwich halves are for them.

In a silent burst of movement they lurch to the side of the Gator where, after a quick sniff, each takes a half sandwich, which they tote a few steps away and wolf down in three quick gulps. Before either Donna or Conner can think to make their escape, the dogs are back upon them — but this time they're happily waltzing around them, weaving in and out, sniffing and nosing at them with languid tongues. And — miracle of miracles — *wagging tails!*

"Does this mean they like us? Or are they just really hungry?" Conner asks, still not moving.

"No. I think we're okay. It's *not* just the moldy roast beef that did it," Donna says, reconsidering the situation. "I realize it now. Dogs are animals of habit. We arrived in a trash truck, which they're familiar with. And we entered the tunnel in the Gator, which they're also familiar with. So, we got here just the way we're supposed to. That makes us less threatening as strangers. But the sandwich didn't hurt."

They eye the animals as the dogs prance around the Gator and watch as one of them happily, disrespectfully inserts his snout deeply into Conner's crotch to get his scent.

"Well, all I can say is, I'm pleased we're within their comfort zone," Conner says quietly, allowing the Doberman to inhale his genetic essence.

"Me too," Donna adds, watching the compromising tableau.

After the dog withdraws his snout and

prances away, Conner joins Donna in the Gator. She steps on the floor pedal, making the miniature truck jolt forward. This excites the dogs and makes them bark for the first time as they happily leap after the intruders. The Gator rolls from the illuminated hothouse back into the sewer culvert, where Conner clicks the remote to lower the noisy garage door behind them. At the end of the culvert they reenter the night air, heavy with the stench of garbage, the hum of the generators on the flatbed truck, and the glow of the single flood lamp atop the pole.

"What now?" Conner asks, watching the dogs run off into the garbage dump.

"What time is it?"

Conner looks at his watch. "Quarter past four."

"Perfect. We've just enough time to stop for coffee at the diner. Then we move on to crime number two." They return to the trash truck and exit the dump. Twice Conner sees the two Dobermans happily trailing after them in the ghostly fog. After they exit the dump, Donna closes the gate and carefully snaps the padlock back into place.

"What role do I play in crime number two?" Conner asks.

"None at all. Not even civilian assist."

"Well, at least tell me where we're going

for you to look into crime number two?"

"Pennsylvania," Donna says. "And *no,* not the Angel Motel."

12
Oops!

Conner Anderson sips coffee and squints with exhaustion at the rural highway where pickup trucks speed by in the morning darkness. They've done this before.

The stringer lights around the windows of the Port J Diner are too bright for this hour, and the worn-out Naugahyde of the booth feels bristly to Conner's skin, which seems to ache with exhaustion.

The waitress arrives with a large tray, narrating each plate as she places them on the table.

"One number-three Mega Morning Breakfast: three scrambled soft with steak, stewed prunes, white toast, and tomato juice for the gentleman; and one number-four Texas Morning Cockcrow: Western omelet with hot sauce and Houston-style beef-sausage patties, quartered-potato home fries, double-thick whole wheat toast, and hand-squeezed OJ for the lady."

Conner breaks the weary silence as he spreads the melted butter on his white toast. "This is a lot more food than I've ever eaten at the crack of dawn."

Donna sips her orange juice and scans the night sky. "I'm hungry," she says, thinking that this is better than her regular breakfast of toasted Eggos. "It's been hours since we had pasta at Napoli Ristorante. And besides, it's still dark. Dawn hasn't cracked yet."

Conner considers the fact that they may be the only couple — ever — who has regular lovers' quarrels without ever having actually made love. "All right," he says. "Let me phrase it differently for Miss Expert Linguist. Why do we have to have such a big breakfast now — *before* the crack of dawn? I'd rather go home and get some sleep. Wouldn't you? I mean, I'm really tired. And crime number two can wait, can't it?"

"No, it cannot," Donna replies matter-of-factly, slicing into her omelet. "Hafez Ozzy Khalal works the morning shift. As they say, 'the early bird flushes the killer.' "

"The guy you phoned from my apartment yesterday? Pretending to be a survey taker?"

"That's the one. But don't get involved. Hush up and eat your eggs. Afterward, we're going to Mr. Khalal's house. Then, depending on some other stuff, we may go back to Dutch Point Nuclear Power Plant."

"Will you promise me that we're not going to get squished by a trash truck this time?"

"There are none so blind as those who fail to observe. Look outside, Vampire Man. What do you see?"

"Oh, yeah. Right."

"That's right. This time — *we're* driving the trash truck and the guy who tried to squish us in your go-cart is in the back, taking a permanent trash nap."

"Yeah, and he must be getting kind of gamy by now," Conner says. After eating in silence for a minute, he speaks again. "So when are we, excuse me, when are *you* going to — as the expression goes — call the cops?"

"Later today. After my fishing trip to Hafez Ozzy Khalal's house. But I'll do it back in the City where the murder occurred. Not up here. The Staties up here are no smarter than the Feds."

"Yeah? Well, like I said last night, what if some other Fibonacci driver sees Jake's truck tooling around up here in the boonies with us driving it instead of Jake? That might not sit too well. It especially might not sit too well if it's Motty or Joe Fibonacci who spots us."

"We'll cross that crisis when we come to it."

Conner considers correcting her ridiculous misquotation; after all, it's the third time she has tortured some trite cliché since they sat down for an early breakfast. But he knows it would annoy her, so he leaves it be, accepting that quotable quotes are not among Donna Prima's strong points. *Hey, isn't that a known mark of true love?*, he wonders — that is, tolerance for your partner's quirks.

And she's right about one thing. He's hungry too. Since leaving the dump, he's found his appetite. Since having dinner at Napoli Ristorante Italiano, he's helped flush a domestic drug gang's delivery and distribution system, witnessed a murder while hiding in a Dumpster, helped locate and explore the upstate hothouse concealed under a mountain of trash where the gang grows and harvests a fortune in pot plants, and come close to being eaten by a pair of hungry Dobermans. *Man-oh-man,* he thinks, digging at his number-three Mega Morning Breakfast, *all that stuff sure will make you hungry.*

"Hey! I remember you two. You had a wager about The Point." It's the waitress who's pouring fresh coffee. They both look up with mouths full of egg and potatoes. "Welcome back. So what's the gamble this morning?"

It's a recognition she'd hoped to avoid.

"And *you*," she says to Conner. "You sure do look like someone on TV. I still can't place it. But give me a minute and I'll come up with it."

They both chew fast and swallow while trying to think of a workable response. Donna gets there first.

"This morning's gamble is whether you get it right."

"How's that?"

"I'm betting the price of our breakfast that you can't name the guy on TV that my partner looks like. *We* know who he looks like. He gets it all the time. But most of the time, people can't place it."

"Take a good look," says Conner, picking up on Donna's lead and smiling at the woman. "If you get it right, she pays for my breakfast. C'mon now, darlin', you gotta help me out."

"Hmmm." She is a tall, high-waisted woman wearing a blue waitress uniform ruffled at the sleeves and covered by a white apron from the waist down. She braces her elbow in her stomach to hold the coffeepot aloft and shifts her weight to her right hip as she ponders Conner's face like a contestant on a game show. Conner's smile widens to a toothy grin. He knows it will not help her recognize him because he never smiles on *Vampire Love Nest*. No one does. It's not allowed. "Well," she says, dabbing her lips with an index finger, "it's just not coming to me. At least not yet. How long do I have?"

"As long as this cup of coffee, which is our last," Donna says. "Then we gotta go."

"Okay. I'll be back." The waitress pours fresh coffee for other early bird diners at nearby tables and returns to the main counter. Conner and Donna nod and shrug. That worked. Even if the waitress guesses right, there's no harm in a person resembling another person. She won't know he's really Conner Anderson, whom she's named as resembling Conner Anderson. They finish their breakfast quickly, but in the process they miss the arrival of a woman who sits at the counter and orders a number six: blueberry Belgian waffles with a double order of sausage links, coffee, and a large grapefruit juice.

Donna and Conner finish their breakfast and amble to the cash register, where the waitress stands chatting with the woman eating blueberry waffles.

"Well, what's it gonna be?" Conner asks. "Which one of us needs to pull out our money?" Before the waitress can respond, the counter customer yodels in an ear-grating soprano.

"Oh my God! It's the two cops from the City. And you, the one who looks like Conner Anderson on *Vampire Love Nest*. How *are* you two?"

She is, of course, the round-faced secretary from the Fibonacci office with the enormous rear end and the Prince Valiant haircut, the one Jake was going to take flying, the one who told Joe Fibonacci of their visit, which resulted in Jake's trying to run them over at Dutch Point, which is one reason he's now compacted in his own truck, which is parked outside in the diner's parking lot.

Once again, Donna and Conner have to think fast, but the waitress thinks faster.

"That's it," she says, pointing at Conner from behind the cash register. "That's it, Esther! *Vampire Love Nest.* I love that show. It's *so* sexy. You look just like one of those sexy vampires who's always biting those zombie women and making love to them."

"Doesn't he?" the secretary screeches in falsetto, jabbing a forkful of blueberry waffle at the actor. "It's just unreal, ha, unreal —

305

no pun intended." She dissolves into high-pitched giggling.

"So, even if I did get help from Esther here," says the waitress, "I still guessed it right."

"That's good enough for me," Donna says, pulling out her wallet to hand over three $10 bills to the waitress. She winks at Conner as though nothing is amiss. "This one is on me."

"Are you still doing EPA work?" the secretary asks. "Hey, that reminds me. That's Jake's truck parked out there. Where is he?"

"Dunno, hon," says the waitress. "I didn't see his shaved-head highness come in this morning. Maybe he went straight to the john."

"Oh, well, in that case he'll be a while." She giggles again in falsetto. "I happen to know from experience that he can spend long chunks of time in the john. But if he comes out soon I'll introduce you to him. He was awfully interested in you both once he heard about your visit last week. I told him all about your driving that little miniature car and everything. And you know, I owe you my appreciation," she says, switching the focus of her chatter to Donna. "I decided to take your advice and accept his invitation."

"Um. . . ." Donna says in a questioning tone, extending her hand to accept change from the waitress, then folding three one-dollar bills in half and handing them back to her as a tip.

"Oh, you remember," the secretary prattles on. "You told me to go ahead, go flying with him in that biplane of his. You were right, of course. As long as we're in the air, he'll just have to keep both hands on the controls — won't he? What's that they call it? A stick? Isn't that what they call the steering wheel in those old planes? Well, as long as he keeps both hands on his stick . . ." She interrupts herself to giggle. ". . . I'll be just fine, won't I?"

All this means only one thing to New York City Police Detective Donna Prima. Just like Jimmy the Nice Bartender, Esther Esterhauser has no idea what those truck-driving thugs are doing. She clearly knows nothing about the hothouse garden inside the Quonset hut buried under a mountain of trash near the light pole. If she did, she'd know Jake the Jerk tried to squash them both. And if she knew that Joe Fibonacci had ordered Jake to be whacked — she'd be alarmed to see his truck parked outside. So she obviously knows nothing. She's innocent. That's good for her and it could be good for the prosecution. Once the lawyers get her on the stand, they'll yank a lifetime of circumstantial evidence from her — providing they can tolerate that braying falsetto.

"Well, ladies, my partner and I need to mosey along. Enjoy your breakfast, Esther."

"Thank you," Esther replies with a mouthful of waffle, holding a greasy sausage in her fingertips. "Oh, but this means you'll miss Jake. I'm sure he'll be coming out of the john any minute now if you can wait."

"Give him our regards," Conner says, edging toward the exit.

They walk slowly through the parking lot.

"Um . . ."

"I know," Donna says quietly, "but don't worry about it. Just get in the truck."

"But . . ."

"No buts. It doesn't matter now."

They climb into the cab of the trash truck as the first crack of dawn emerges over the Gas & Delly Mart opposite the Port J Diner. As Donna cranks the engine, the waitress sees them while taking an order from another booth in the front window. She turns and calls out toward the counter. A moment later Esther Esterhauser waddles to the window, where she stands next to the waitress, watching slack-jawed as Conner and Donna drive Jake's truck from its oversized parking space, around a loop toward the front, and directly past the row of windows in front of the diner. The last thing either of them sees of the secretary is the little opened "O" of a mouth in Esther's plump, perfectly round face. They make a right turn out of the parking lot toward Port Juttistown, the Walmart, and Dutch Point Nuclear Power Plant and drive through the woods to the Angel Bridge that crosses the Delaware River to Los Angeles, Pennsylvania.

13
HAFEZ OZZY KHALAL

The house sits on Angel Road just a mile from the Angel Motel on the bank of the Delaware River in Los Angeles, Pennsylvania across the river from, and a little north of, Port Juttistown, New York. Little more than an ordinary, suburban, three-bedroom ranch, it is built on buttressed landfill rising high atop the Pennsylvania side of the riverbank. But it *does* have a killer view of the Delaware River. Then again, on the downside, it also sits almost directly above that ridiculously big sign reading:

Los Angeles, Pa.
The True City of Angels

Donna parks the truck in a turnout a little beyond the house along the narrow two-lane highway similar to the one in New York State where they were almost smushed the previous week.

"Dutch Point is only about a quarter mile up river. Looks like my man lives close enough to row a boat to work."

"Your suspect lives in that house? Nice view, but who'd want to look at that ugly sign down there all day and night? It must be as big as the Hollywood sign in Hollywood."

Donna turns off the engine and pulls back the emergency brake handle. "Yeah, that's what you call stupid supreme," she says. "I ought to put a picture of it in my book."

"The more I get to know you — the more I want to read your book."

"Maybe I'll dedicate it to you." She reaches to her ankle to check the position of her pink .38.

"What an honor — to have a book about stupidity dedicated to me." Whenever he speaks sarcastically, his Southern accent is stronger and more amusing. Donna must force herself not to laugh.

"Okay, listen!" she barks, putting on her tough cop voice and sawing the air with both hands. It's a tone and a gesture that he has come to understand. It means he's not the boyfriend — at least not at the present moment, not while she's doing *real* work as a *real* cop. "It's almost time for this joker to go to his job on the early shift. I'm going to go up there and knock on his door. I may go inside. I may not. Your job is to stay here in the truck and stay out of trouble. Got it? If you come across any empty Dumpsters sitting around — do not, I repeat *do not* climb into them."

Conner is aching tired and does not feel like challenging any aspect of her pushy copitude. He salutes in mock obedience. "Yes, ma'am!"

She opens the door and swings both legs out to climb down from the cab of the trash truck.

"What about a good-bye kiss?" Conner asks.

Donna stops. She slowly looks back at him. It's only the second time he's ever seen her arching eyebrow. Unlike the last time, it relaxes almost immediately and falls back into its proper place above her right eye. She leans sideways to kiss him on the lips. It's only the second time their lips have even met, and it comes with a pleasant wrinkle of goosebumps down his spine.

"Be careful, honey," Conner says as Donna slides down from the cab, stepping onto the running board and slamming the door shut.

Honey!

The nerve, she thinks, crossing the rural

highway to Hafez Ozzy Khalal's front door. *The next thing you know he'll want me to rub his feet.* She makes a mental note to tell him never to call her that again . . . never . . . uh . . . but then, for reasons she can't explain — she rips up the mental note.

She walks through the driveway, where a late-model convertible Ford Mustang is parked. It's light orange with dark red pinstripe scroll stretching the length of both sides. The retractable hood is black. *It's the American dream,* Donna thinks. It's different for everyone. And most of the time it's very easy to spot. For this man, paradise is a house in America with a river view and a muscle car parked out front.

She examines the registration and inspection stickers, the body, plates, and tires, then feels the hood — it's cold. The front lawn is small and well cared for. A statuesque brown rabbit sits under a shrub near the porch, which Donna thinks to be a cheesy lawn ornament until it darts from under the greenery and sprints a zigzag pattern across the yard in the morning sun. It disappears in the thick wooded undergrowth next to the house. While on the job, she's startled plenty of dogs and rats who let her know they were unhappy with her presence. There was even a ferret once — but never a rabbit, which makes that little guy her first.

The porch is a cramped platform with barely enough room for the storm door to swing open. She rings the doorbell and immediately hears footfall approaching. She stands inside the opened storm door, bracing it with her foot. A shadow appears at the small door window followed by the unlatching and opening of the inner door.

"Good morning, sir. My name is Detective Prima of the New York City Police Department." She holds her badge aloft just long enough for it to have the desired effect, then reattaches the clip to her belt. "I'm working a case in the City that you may be able to help me with. Are you Hafez Khalal?"

"Yes."

"Is that your Mustang, sir?"

"Yes."

"Is it registered in your name?"

"Yes."

"May I come in and speak with you, sir?"

The vehicle has nothing to do with anything. It's something they teach in cadet school. Get 'em accustomed to saying the word "yes." Get 'em to say "Yes," "Sure," and "Yes, ma'am," several times in quick succession so that by time they'd otherwise say "No," they'll be less inclined to do so.

It's a neat trick and it usually works.

The problem is — Hafez Khalal is not saying "Yes." He's pausing to consider the situation. The pause is followed by the normal catch in the throat, nervous eyes, even a hint of beading sweat. It's a reaction familiar to all cops. The problem is — you could stop a perfectly innocent stranger on the street and play with his head by acting like a tough cop and get the exact same response. The trick is — get past the initial nervousness before allowing your instincts to draw conclusions. But then again, Khalal didn't fall for the "Yes" trick. She asks again.

"May I come in and speak with you, sir?"

"I have to go to work. What's this about?" He looks pretty much the way she pictured him: average height and weight, short hair, brown eyes, medium complexion, easy to look at, intelligent looking. He also has a silly little Clark Gable-style mustache. *This guy may be a Syrian Arab, but with the house, car, and mustache, he's morphed into pure American,* she thinks.

"Well, sir, it won't take much time. I'd be happy to tell you about it if you invite me in?" He still hesitates. Donna decides to hike the tone of the conversation a couple of cop-notches. "All right, sir, how about this — how about you step outside if you don't want to invite me in? Step right down here in the yard and we'll talk there. Does that work for you?"

She releases the storm door and steps backward, down the two steps of the small porch. He follows, leaving the inner door ajar. The storm door swooshes shut.

"Sir, I'm investigating a crime that took place in New York City almost one year ago." She pauses to look at him, let the silence make him nervous.

Nothing.

"It took place in Greenwich Village, on Leroy Street."

Hmm, maybe that was something, maybe nothing. It could have been a little twitch of fear. Right about now he's thinking about yesterday's phone call, trying to match her voice with the voice on the phone. Okay, here comes the bomb.

"I'm talking about the murder of Mustapha Zizira, a Syrian national working as a cook at King Falafel."

Twitch!

No question about it. That was a twitch. He's not only worried about her; he's also worried about himself — about whether he can keep up the pretense and for how long. It can be a complex poker game or it can be child's play to break a guilty man trying to bluff his way past a street cop. It all depends on how much steel is in the suspect's bones. There's also the female factor. These Muslim types don't like being pushed around by a woman. But if he comes back at her with anger — it'll likely be only an artifice to help him keep up his charade, phony emotion to help him bluster past his own agitation as he concludes that her voice *is* the voice of the mysterious caller.

"Uh . . ." His worry bubbles up through his voice. "I don't know anything about. . . ."

All right — time for the secret weapon, even if it is a lie.

"Mr. Khalal — at this time I need to inform you that I have irrefutable evidence linking you to one Sabeen Abbasi of Duluth, Minnesota, where you went to college on a student visa. That woman is now Mrs. Mustapha Zizira, the widow of the man murdered a year ago on the morning of August 28 while in the kitchen of King Falafel, where he was baking a tray of baklava."

"Uh. . . ."

He moves so fast even Donna is surprised. Hafez Khalal bounds up the small front stoop, yanks open the storm door, and plunges into the house. His speed reminds her of one of those programs about prey

and predator on The Animal Channel —
the ones that show rodents with hyped-up
metabolisms that can fire their rockets the
instant they get a whiff of the fox or the
bobcat or see the shadow of the owl coming
in for a landing.

There's no point in calling out for him to
stop. He's gone. She unholsters her pink
snubbie and enters the house cautiously. A
rumbling sound in the back of the house is
followed by the loud clomp of racing footsteps and the opening and closing of the
back door. Moving now with her own speed,
Donna lets go of all caution and rushes to
follow the noises through the living room,
dining room, and kitchen, out the back door
and into the rear yard, which slopes steeply
down a wooded terrain to the river below.
There's no sign of Khalal on the hillside.

Whirr-whirr-whirr-varoom.

The Mustang! He's in the Mustang.

She runs to the side of the house and back
to the front yard as he backs out of the
driveway. His left hand extends from the
window.

Merda! Is that a frigging gun?

POP!

*Yes, that would definitely be a gun. That
creep is actually* shooting *at me.*

She dives nose first into the grass of the

well-manicured lawn. The noise comes again.

POP!

Donna runs down her choices. She can stay down. She can get up and run away. Or she can shoot back. She chooses the third option. Staying prone, she braces on both elbows and fires one shot just as Khalal completes backing up and shifts the Mustang into forward gear. Her bullet hits the small rear window, instantly turning it into a pattern of concentric cracks. Khalal responds by firing one more shot . . .

POP . . . and floors the accelerator, which makes the tires burn rubber and send two parallel clouds of smoke rising from the asphalt under the rear wheels.

Prima knows that he'll be gone in two seconds, just as when he darted into the house. There's only one thing to do, so she does it.

POP . . . POP . . . POP . . . POP.

She empties her pink revolver at the Mustang, which appears unfazed as it begins to pick up speed — the spinning rear wheels biting into asphalt.

Uh-HOOO-gah-h-h.

It's the truck! Having witnessed the shoot-out, Conner has cranked the truck engine and lays on the ahooga horn as he maneu-

319

vers onto the highway to block the path of the escaping Mustang. Khalal spins to the narrow shoulder to scoot past, but Conner bears down, catching the orange muscle car by the rear end, smashing it on the right rear fender like a squeezebox and pinning it to the shoulder grade. Khalal opens the door, which jams into the dirt, giving him barely enough room to shimmy past. Unaware that Donna is out of bullets, he fires one shot at her, ducks, and races up the grade and into the woods. Donna holsters her weapon and runs to the truck.

"Good thinking. Quick, toss me that SIG Sauer from the glove box." Conner does so. She catches the fancy automatic, racks the first bullet into the chamber, and races up the shoulder grade and into the thick undergrowth that leads down to the rapidly flowing Delaware River.

In the woods, there's no sign of the fugitive, but that's not an issue for Donna. It's clear enough that he's running down the sloping terrain to the river. Maybe he has a canoe or a kayak tied up down there. If so, and if he gets to it, he'll probably get away. But even that is not an issue. For her, the only real issue is — do not let this guy lay up behind some tree to wait for her — then shoot her. She may be from Bensonhurst, but she's also a cop and in this scenario there isn't much difference between trees in the woods and parked cars in the hood. Donna slows down. There's a broken bush branch and beyond it some tamped-down ferns. She eases her way along, stooping, hoping to catch sight of Khalal in the distance to be certain he's not lying for her. Ten feet ahead there's a distinct opening in a thick batch of Queen Anne's lace, a narrow path that breaks through the clusters of bouncing knee-high white blossoms. She goes to the path, kneels, and bobs up like a jack-in-the-box, straining her eyes for a glimpse of anything that moves. She looks for a boat, but the letters of the giant sign obscure her view of the riverbank.

There — almost at the river! He must be crawling to avoid being seen. The undergrowth down by the riverbank is waving. The tips of the foliage bounce like a warning flag as Khalal bulldozes on his belly toward the water's edge. That's it. He's not lying in wait for her. Donna stands up and races down the steep wooded incline, turning sideways where necessary for better footing while keeping a watch on the still-waving undergrowth as she descends.

At twenty feet away she stops near the huge sign in an open area near the riverbank and aims the SIG Sauer upstream at the moving foliage. The flowing water is noisy. *Steady, steady now, just hold position.* He'll be emerging any second. She has enough time to breathe and think about what to say when he crawls from the undergrowth. "Drop it!" Nah, too predictable. "Freeze, you lowlife." Too sappy. How about — "Don't move or I'll kill you, Mr. Khalal." Yeah, that works. It has a kind of 007 ring to it. Even Conner would approve.

POP!

The bullet whizzes past her head. Donna spins.

There he is!

He's standing in shallow water next to a kayak buffeting against his legs in the current. What's he doing over there? And she's standing in the open — a stationary target in a shooting gallery. Donna jumps backward to safety before he can get off another shot. By standing behind the letter "l," the next-to-last letter in the series of letters that spells "Los Angeles, Pa, The True City of Angels," she's protected, at least temporarily.

But wait a minute. If he's in the water — what's that moving around in the foliage? She doesn't have to wait for an answer. The shot Khalal fired has frightened the bear

cub, sending it bolting from the undergrowth, disoriented and squealing madly.
It's a small bear, but not so small its teeth
couldn't do serious harm. Both Donna and
Khalal are startled by the sudden intruder,
whose noisy panic demonstrates its extreme
state of agitation. In his confusion the bear
heads straight for Khalal, who turns his
weapon away from Donna behind the letter
"l" and toward the furry beast.

*Well, if he's going to shoot the bear cub,
this is her chance to shoot him. That's not a
bad deal.*

She leans to the side of the letter "l" and
takes steady aim. There's no need to say
anything. There's no time for clever cop
warnings. Once he shoots the cub, he'll spin
back to her and empty his chamber. Her
index finger tightens down on the trigger of
the SIG Sauer.

Merda! Che cazzo fai?

Just as Donna is set to fire a nine-
millimeter bullet into Khalal's chest, the
knee-deep water behind him suddenly boils
with whitecaps as though a monster is rising from the ocean depths and lunging
toward him.

Che diavolo fai?

Feeling and hearing the approaching
danger, Khalal spins to see what's going on

just as the huge black bear, standing erect on two legs directly behind him, swings one giant paw, landing the blow on Khalal's head and sending him careening over the top of his kayak. Quaking with hostility, the bear snorts loudly at Khalal's legs as they fly past. It grips an ankle, bites down ferociously, and hoists the entire man, upside down, from the water and flings him aside into deeper water.

With Khalal out of the way, the bear returns to all fours and trots through the water to meet the still panicky cub at the riverbank, where it quickly sniffs the baby from nostril to anus until satisfied that all is well. The adult bear looks back at Khalal, who is left gasping for air and grimacing in pain in waist-deep water rapidly turning red all around him. Satisfied that no more violence is necessary, the mama bear noses her baby to move down the riverbed, away from the nasty man.

Madre di Dio.

Conner is never going to believe this. Nobody is ever going to believe it. Mama bear was in the river fishing for trout while baby bear was left alone to frolic on the shore, and Khalal hadn't seen either one. Well, as they teach you in the Girl Scouts and as all hunters know — never get be-

tween a mother bear and her cub. Hafez
Ozzy Khalal has just learned that lesson the
hard way.

■ ■ ■ ■

PART FOUR:
KAH-CHUNK!

■ ■ ■ ■

1
HEY, THANKS, MR. MAYOR

"Make no mistake about it. The dedication and courage of this detective is a perfect example of why we refer to the NYPD as 'New York's finest' and it is the essence of what makes this city so great."

Donna has always found the Mayor's whiny voice to be grating to the ears. But in this instance, she's wonderfully happy to listen to his nasal drone as he compliments her on the steps of City Hall.

The steps of City Hall!

This ceremony was considered so important, it was moved outside from the Blue Room, where mayoral news conferences and boring formal announcements are normally made.

This is one aspect of Tetris going *kah-chunk* that she never dreamed could happen. She'd dreamed some pretty farfetched stuff. But this? Of course, the man speaking from the podium *is* running for re-election for a fifth term, so he's looking to share all the good-news spotlight he can get.

"She . . . was . . . relentless," the mayor drones on, "and for that, our city is a safer place today. Not only did this intrepid detective voluntarily work on her own time, staking out a murderous drug gang operating in both our city and upstate, but she also took the initiative to set up a drug bust in a Greenwich Village liquor store, ultimately resulting in the arrest of no less than two dozen suspects operating at all levels of a multi-million-dollar marijuana supply and distribution chain. That bust also shut down a Mob-run company that utilized privately owned trash trucks to make deliveries throughout the tri-state area. And . . . oh yes . . . in the process of doing all that — she also made an arrest on an unrelated, one-year-old murder that was on the verge of becoming lost among the city's cold-case files. And in *that* case, her crime-fighting partner was a 400-pound New York State black bear. Ladies and gentlemen — this is one helluva cop!"

Santa Madre!

Then there has been the media coverage. The papers have been running the story with her photo all week. The *Daily News* front page read:

Lady Detective with Pink Gun
Busts Hothouse Pot Dump

The *Post* headline read:

Pink Pistol Hot Cop
Bops Pot Thugs

Two days later, the *New York Times* headline took a different tack. It read:

NYPD Firearm Violation
Overlooked After Detective Solves
High-Profile Crimes

That article began:

Some are calling it an unprecedented exemption in the history of the New York City Police Department.

Whether that is true or not, no one disagrees that police brass are overlooking a violation of departmental firearm rules in the case of an NYPD Detective who possesses a hot-pink firearm.

It is the storied adventure of Detective Maria-Donatella Prima who, earlier this week, single-handedly busted a multimillion-dollar drug ring suspected of several murders. Her pink .38 Smith & Wesson is a blatant violation of department firearm regulations. Yet the Police Commissioner has called her willingness to break the rules "The very reason why she is now the finest of the finest."

Some officers, however, are grumbling behind the scenes, arguing that such a violation should not be allowed. They say it is being tolerated, even sanctioned in this case, only because Detective Prima has suddenly drawn national attention with her daring exploits. And some say the mayor, who is running for his fifth term in office, has privately told police brass to back off.

Likening it to a dispensation from the Pope, they complain . . .

"You told me there were no rules against having a pink gun," Conner had said, after reading the *Times* article.

"No, I didn't."

"Well, I thought you did."

"Well, I didn't. The only thing I told you was that I bought it online and that no wisecracks were allowed. And that still goes."

"Is it what you got punished for?" he'd asked. "You know, the thing that put you on desk duty?"

"No, that is not what I got punished for.

The reason for that is none of your business. It's water under the sewer. So don't ever ask again. It's only between me and Captain Hurly. Got it?"

"Okay, okay. I got it. Geesh!"

It has been going on all week. The media have been everywhere. And they're all making a very big deal of her pink snubnose .38. The photogs have all demanded a shot of it on her ankle after they got a photo of her. Camera crews have been waiting on the street at her Bensonhurst apartment building in the morning to follow her to work at the Sixth Precinct. Some even followed her to the local deli and reported to the world that her favorite sandwich is smoked turkey on rye with honey mustard. Even her father's photo appeared in the *Daily News* after she cited her retired firefighter dad as her inspiration and mentor, always encouraging her to work hard on behalf of the City of New York — the land where her forebears settled after arriving from Calabria.

"Calabria is the toe of the boot that kicks the Sicilian ball," Tony Prima told the tabloid reporter who knocked on his door in Bensonhurst. "So who do you think is tougher — Calabrese or Sicilian?"

Good old Dad. What a great guy!

The mayor's droning continues on the steps of City Hall.

"That Mob-run trash company, by the way, was previously investigated by the FBI and given a clean bill of health as being fully law abiding," he says, taking a swipe at the Bureau, which only endears him to her NYPD heart more than ever. "The Feds missed what New York Detective Donna Prima ultimately uncovered. They couldn't see it for looking at it. It took a New York City cop to make the big bust."

Oh stop, please, you're killing me. Grazie, dolce Gesù.

Donna is standing behind the mayor and is flanked by the police chief and the first deputy commissioner on one side and by the chief of the department and chief of detectives on the other.

Santa Madre, there's more brass standing on these steps than you could find on a fleet of battleships.

While the mayor whines on with his overly long atta-boy, she scans the audience. There's Dad — front-row center, happily nodding at the mayor's words. There's Mom sitting next to him, her face aglow with pride. They're surrounded by her two brothers, sisters-in-law, and even Aunt Mary.

Aunt Mary, please stop flirting with that guy

in front of you — he must be 70 years old and he's way too young for you.

Behind them sit Captain Bill Hurly; Detective Tony Sporietto, who's back from vacation; Officers Cicarelli, Giangola, and Sullivan; and half of the entire police force from the Sexy Sixth.

Hey, did Cicarelli just wink at me? That low-life. I'll take care of him later.

She has no idea who the rest of the crowd is. There's the media — corralled onto a riser platform in the back. There's a crowd of curious New Yorkers allowed in from the street and forced to stand behind blue police barricades. But who are all these other dressed-up people with seats, and why are they here? They look like they've all got money, like wine-drinking, air-kissing types.

Oh yeah — they must be friends of the mayor, which means they really are wine-drinking, air-kissing types.

She continues to scan the crowd, finally finding the man she's looking for. He's sitting near the back row, behind a lady with a stupid Easter Parade hat. Donna makes eye contact with Conner, who beams at her and gives a thumbs up, which makes her smile in return.

Hey, Vampire Man, believe it or not — you have been the best part of this whole champi-

onship round of Tetris.

"And so, without further ado, let me ask New York City Police Detective Maria-Donatella Prima to step forward to the podium. In recognition of your services and on behalf of a grateful city — please accept this Medal of Honor, the highest law-enforcement award given by the City's police department."

Okay, sure. Why not?

"In addition, I am proud to present you with your new badge, the gold shield designating you as Detective-Investigator, and of course the promotion comes with a pay increase commensurate with a job well done."

Oh yeah, baby.

"Congratulations, Detective Prima."

"Thank you, Mr. Mayor."

Kah-chunk!

2
GEE, THAT'S TOO BAD

"Special Agent Holm speaking."

"Good morning, Agent Holm. This is Detective-Investigator Donna Prima with the NYPD calling."

"Oh. Yes. Good morning." She can hear it in his voice. She's one of the last people this G-man wants to speak with.

"I've phoned to say thank you for your help on the Zizira murder case and the arrest of Hafez Khalal in Port Juttistown. Your Q&A with Samir, you remember — the man who owns King Falafel — well, that helped me plug a line into Khalal as a suspect. It turned out to be an ordinary revenge killing by a spurned lover. During my investigation last year, his wife lied to me, saying she had no previous boyfriends before her husband. So I want to acknowledge your help and express my appreciation to you and to the Bureau."

"Oh . . . uh . . . yes. Well, you know I only

got tapped that morning by Special Agent Wilson. I had nothing better to do, so I just rode along as shotgun. I was in New York at the time for a meeting on improving inter-departmental communication channels."

"I see. Well, I thank you just the same. I'm going to call Special Agent Wilson next and thank him too."

"Well, you're going to have to reach him in a different field office."

"Oh? Did he get bumped up to work with you in Washington?"

"No, he got transferred to Thermopolis, Wyoming."

"Never heard of it. And I didn't know there was an FBI bureau in such a place."

"There wasn't. But there is now. And he's it."

"I see. Well, it's none of my business, but maybe you can tell me — what happened to the case involving missing nuclear stuff from Dutch Point?"

There is a long pause before Holm answers.

"Detective Prima, you didn't hear it from me, okay? But I'll tell you. It wasn't missing."

"Excuse me?"

"It wasn't missing. Nothing was actually stolen. The whole thing was a mistake, some sort of inventory miscount. When they recounted — it was all there. Every bit of it. That, and the narco bust in his own backyard after he had formally given Fibonacci a clean bill — well, let's just say Wilson is lucky to even be in Wyoming."

"I see." She can hardly contain herself — so much for assignments from the *very highest authority.*

Kah-chunk!

3
VASILY LEONID PUTSKAYA

The mid-afternoon traffic in this extreme northern part of Astoria, Queens, seems noisier than anything in Manhattan. There are just too many panel trucks and delivery vans. They're all loading up on goods for the second shipment of the day to companies in Manhattan. These guys are the middlemen between the suppliers and the grocery stores and restaurants.

Queens has always been Donna's third favorite borough, after Brooklyn and Manhattan. The Bronx is fourth and Staten Island — a/k/a Copland — is last on the list. Staten Island is where cops go after they get married and start punching out kids. Bah. You have to take the Verrazano to get to Copland, and the Brooklyn Bridge is the only bridge she's ever going to cross to go home at night.

Donna parks her unmarked car on Steinway Street two blocks from The Markham

House and walks past the messy clutter of auto-body shops, small trucking outfits, and micro-manufacturing operations. The building façades all have a look that reflects the neighborhood's history of factory labor. Many neighborhoods in other boroughs tell similar stories with hundred-year-old industrial buildings that used to employ thousands of brawny men but are now gentrified apartment buildings.

Vasily Leonid Putskya has been a no-show at his job as a day laborer for a moving van company for the past week. And, interestingly, in the past week there have been burglaries at one apartment in Chelsea and two on the Upper West Side, where Starrhouse Moving Company was contracted to load up or unload a customer. Clever. That means he has an accomplice on the van. He's meeting him at the buildings and going in with the other movers. After hitting an apartment where nobody's home, he waltzes past the doorman with a load of stolen jewelry in his pockets without arousing any suspicion. That's even better than having a partner on the street. This way, he has an *inside* partner.

The Markham House is a converted former something-or-other, not much wider than a townhouse. The architecture has a look about it that says Polish or Ukrainian. In the nineteenth century it was probably a school for some particular ethnicity, or maybe it was a community hall for some immigrant group that needed assistance resettling in the new world. Whatever it was, it wasn't called The Markham House in those days.

The lobby smells like last week's pot roast with sauerkraut. The man at the front desk has the distinctive round face and short muscular body of an ethnic Russian. Donna unclips her badge from her belt and leans near the counter to display it, but without touching anything. There's something about not touching anything that says "I am a cop and I am in charge."

"I'm Detective Prima with the NYPD. Are you Gennadi?"

"Yes."

"I spoke with you this morning. Has Putskya returned to his room?"

"No. He's still out."

"Good. I have a search warrant here." She gestures to her pocket as if to withdraw the document, but pauses, her hand poised over her hip.

"Yes, yes," Gennadi says, waving it off as unnecessary. "Do you have a key?"

"No! No, I do not have a key," she barks

with cop anger. "How would I have a key?"

Her attitude immediately produces the desired results.

"Okay, okay. I give you master key."

"Right. And what room is it?"

"Room eight. Floor two." He gestures to the rear of the building. "The back."

"Right. Okay, listen, Gennadi. If Putskya comes in while I'm up there, do not say anything to him. Do not tip him off. Understand? Just let him pass by. Let him go up to his room. Got it?"

He gives a big shoulder shrug and purses his lips. "Yah. Sure. Okay."

Donna makes certain he's looking her in the eye. "Right. Just let him go up." Once she's satisfied that Gennadi gets the message, she breaks eye contact, then turns and walks up the narrow staircase to the second floor. She gives a reassuring glance at her pants cuff, which conceals her pink snubbie, which is fully loaded with five .357 +p hollowpoint bullets.

The door to room eight reminds Donna of the hundred-year-old door on Conner's apartment in the Village. And there's a wobbly yield in the frame, which allows her to peek inside. A shaft of dark sunlight falls across a tall twin mattress bed frame, disheveled with a dirty pillow and blanket.

Dirty laundry is scattered across the floor. No need to draw her revolver — nobody's home in this rat trap.

She inserts the master key, unlocks the useless bolt, steps inside, then closes the door behind her and relocks it. In addition to the bed, there's one ancient looking ladder-back chair, one rickety table, and two suitcases on the floor. That's it. There's no bureau, no closet, no bathroom, and the one window has a burglar-proof security gate bolted over it. *Some prison cells are more cozy than this dump,* Donna thinks.

Well, if there's any evidence in here — it's going to be in the suitcases. They're both made of cheap electric blue plastic that's supposed to imitate leather. She flips open the nearest one with her foot — more dirty laundry, lots of T-shirts and things with the Yankees logo. There's also a baseball glove, a first baseman's mitt signed by Don Mattingly. *There it is,* Donna thinks. That's his American paradise: baseball in general and the Yankees in particular. He probably harbors fantasies of playing pro ball, which isn't logical because he's Russian. After chess and vodka, isn't soccer their main sport? Besides, how many Russians have ever been tapped to play for the major leagues? And he probably stole the autographed glove anyway. Well, at least there are no signs of drugs. No needles, crack vials, or pot paraphernalia are lying around.

She closes the flap and steps behind the bed to flip open the other suitcase with her foot.

Ta-da.

That's why half his dirty laundry is lying all over the floor. This other suitcase is filled with stolen goods: several GPS devices, half a dozen iPods, bunches of shiny little compact cameras, a couple of hunting knives, and a big Swiss Army knife with all the attached gizmos including the corkscrew and little toothpick. There's even a stun gun that looks like a Norelco electric shaver.

There are also two stuffed toiletry bags. She picks up the first one and dumps its contents near the foot of the bed.

Watches! Men's and women's watches of all styles. She thumbs through them. They're mostly middle-of-the-road stuff, nothing fancy. If this guy ever stole a Rolex, he didn't bother keeping it here. There's also a collection of small Fabergé eggs. Well, that would attract his interest considering he's Russian, but to Donna they appear made of cheap glass and she doubts they have much value.

She picks up the other toiletry bag, which

is smaller and lighter. Unzipping it, she dumps the contents at the opposite end of the mattress, near the head.

Jewelry! Rings, necklaces, brooches, bracelets, and earrings. Most of it appears cheap and a little gaudy. Costume crap from the Macy's counter in the middle of the main floor. The good stuff would have been sold already — fenced to some crook on 47th Street.

Donna thumbs through the pile, plucking out the stringy necklaces with doodads that dangle noisily, separating them out from the smaller stuff. *Why do women do this to themselves?* she wonders. Jewelry and war paint are two things she's never had a liking for. Why do women think they need pearls or eye shadow? All a woman really needs to be a woman is a brain and — in her case — a pink pistol.

From the second pile she separates all cuff links and masculine-looking rings. In that smaller pile of men's jewelry, she's looking for one ring in particular.

Well, what do you know. Grazie, Signore Putskya.

Donna slides the ring into her pocket just as she hears loud footsteps rapidly coming down the hallway — footsteps that make squeaking noises, which tell her the walker is wearing sneakers. She adjusts the blanket to cover the two piles of jewelry on the bed. The door rattles loudly as the key is inserted and the bolt turns over.

Vasily Leonid Putskya enters his room hastily and flips on the light. He drops his backpack, sits on the ladder-back chair, and unlaces his Nike Air Jordans. Kneeling out of sight on the opposite side of the bed and looking under the bed frame, Donna can see his hands tug at the backpack. He unzips it and begins pulling out the contents, fumbling with them as he does so. A watch drops to the floor, followed by an iPhone and a man's leather wallet.

Donna quietly unholsters her pink .38, braces herself, and springs to an erect stance from the opposite side of the bed, her weapon pointing directly at the suspect.

"Police! Get on the floor!"

Putskya is so startled he bounces in the chair as though stunned with a Taser. He stares at her with a gaping mouth.

"I said get on the floor!" Donna shouts as she maneuvers around the end of the bed to a position directly in front of him so she can cuff him when he goes down. "Down! Now!"

But Putskya does not move. He is still too surprised to comprehend what is being shouted at him. He stares back at her and at the short barrel of the pink .38 revolver aimed at his chest. Donna takes in his full appearance: male-white, short brown hair, pimples, about 20 years old, slender build, 5'9", 140 pounds.

"Speak English, pal? I said 'Down!' Now!"

Instead of getting down, Putskya does the unthinkable. He stands up.

What? What does he think he's doing? I hope this guy is not contemplating suicide by cop.

Donna backs away and squares her feet, getting ready to shoot if he lunges at her. But Putskya does not lunge. He just stands there, calmly looking very carefully at the revolver. One of his pimples is a large cyst with a bulging whitehead near the corner of his mouth.

"Yeah, it's real," she shouts. "It's a real gun, if that's what you're wondering."

Putskya removes his eyes from the .38 only long enough to look Donna up and down from head to toe. When he's finished, he looks at her straight on and speaks in a thick Russian accent with the most contemptuous tone of voice she's ever heard.

"Your lee-tul gun is pink — like pussy," he grunts.

She lowers the .38, rears back with her

right arm, and slams her fist into his mouth, knocking him backward into the ladder-back chair, which breaks into a dozen pieces. She grips his thick leather belt above his butt, drags him from the pile of sticks, kicks his legs apart, drops a knee into the small of his back, and pulls both arms behind him to receive the cuffs.

He's only half conscious when she turns him over, his eyes rolling as he tries to focus. The whitehead pimple near his mouth has burst from the force of the blow. A spot of blood runs down his chin.

"How old are you, Putskya?" she asks.

He groans. Donna shakes him by the neck. "How old?"

"21," he says slowly.

"21. Well that's good. Because I am going to tell you something that you can put to good use for the rest of your life. That is — once you get out of jail. Understand? *Understand?*" she shouts a second time, shaking him again when he does not respond.

Putskya nods.

"Good. Here it is. Never, *ever* speak to any woman in that insulting manner ever again. Got it?" When he does not respond, Donna shakes him forcefully by the neck. "I said 'Do you understand?' "

"Yes," he mumbles quickly in his thick

Russian accent, still feeling the pain of the blow and the fall to the floor. "Yes. I apologize." Donna pats him on the face with her open palm.

"Much better."

Kah-chunk!

4
AWW, THAT'S SO SWEET

Donna makes the presentation to Conner while sitting, as they did that first night, on the foot of his brass bed in his tiny bedroom with the window overlooking Eighth Avenue. It's his last night in the walk-up apartment. In the morning, he moves around the corner to a doorman building on Horatio Street.

He is thrilled with the gift, like a small boy in a Norman Rockwell illustration of Christmas morning.

"Oh, you did it. You really did it. My dad's college ring!" His eyes fill with tears as he kisses her forehead and high cheekbones. "Thank you, thank you." He rolls the cherished gold ring around his little finger, looking at the minute scrollwork. "Look, you see there, it says *Ole Miss, Class of '69.*"

"Yeah," Donna says. "That's why I plucked it from the scumbag's stash. Because I saw it's from . . . down yonder in

Dixieland." She tries to affect a saccharine Southern accent, but as usual mangles the job. "You know, good ole Mississippi." Conner is set to burst with a second round of kisses and "Thank you's" when he stops suddenly.

"Hey, hold on there, Pink Pistol Lady. What about my scumbag's execution by guillotine in Times Square? You promised."

"Oh yeah. Hang on." She reaches into her hip pocket, trying to avoid kneeing the poster of Laurence Olivier emoting over Yorick's skull, which is wrapped in corrugated cardboard for safe transfer during the move around the corner to Horatio Street. She withdraws a folded piece of paper and hands it to him.

"What's this?"

"After that big ceremony on the steps of City Hall, Mayor Mike asked me if there was anything else he could do. So I called in a little favor. Go ahead, unfold it."

Conner opens the paper and smiles, revealing the protruding incisors of the vampire biteplate inserted in his mouth.

"I asked him to draw a scumbag lying on a guillotine," Donna continues, "but he said he could only do a hangman, so you'll have to settle for this, Vampire Man."

"Then I'll have to accept a scumbag get-

ting hanged instead of a scumbag getting
guillotined," says Conner with a happy
smile, his prominent vampire incisors protruding as he kisses her again, this time on
the lips. "And thank you for the ring, Pink
Pistol Lady."

"You're welcome, Vampire Man."

He kisses her again. "And thank you for
letting me be secret partner to New York's
hottest cop in The Case of the Hothouse
Pot Dump."

"You're welcome, Vampire Man."

He kisses her again. "And thank you for my hangman art drawn and signed by the Mayor."

"You're welcome, Vampire Man."

"And thank you for keeping your pink pistol strapped to your ankle."

"You're welcome, Vampire Man."

He leans back to bare his vampire fangs and slowly moves his teeth to her neck. "And thank you for . . ."

"Ah-h-h . . . yes! You're welcome, Vampire Man."

Kah-chunk!

ACKNOWLEDGMENTS

The author wishes to express appreciation to Christian Alighieri, Charles Salzberg, Lisa Weiss, Ginny Kosola and Ray McNally, Bruce Goldstone, Michael Neff and my writer colleagues at the 2010 Algonkian Conference in New York City: Henry Oksman, Barry Fields, Mary Curran, Arnold Wolf, Tom Lowery, David Sanders, Lisa Dewar, Marti Green, Jeff Lee, Tom Kenis, Chris Divver, Tammy Narayan, Mary Wright, David Jubinville, Shyam Mehta.

ACKNOWLEDGMENTS

ABOUT THE AUTHOR

After almost three decades as a New York radio newswriter, editor, and reporter, **Gray Basnight** is now deeply immersed in fiction writing. *The Cop with the Pink Pistol* is his debut novel. Gray lives in New York City with his wife, Lisa Weiss. For more information, visit **www.graybasnight.com.** You can reach Gray at **graybasnight@gmail .com.**